Words. Words. Words. Pressing up from her stomach, trembling on her lips. Words buzzing in her throat like caught bees. Banging in her head. Harsh words. Angry words. Sounds boiling up in her like sap. Wild things she couldn't let out.

Yow! A kick from her brother almost caused Omakayas to blurt an exclamation.

No! Omakayas sealed her lips together in a firm line and glared at her brother with all of the force pent up inside. If the fire from her eyes could scorch him, Pinch would be the first to yell out. Then he would lose the game of silence.

ALSO BY LOUISE ERDRICH

LOUISE ERDRICH

THE GAME OF SILENCE

HarperTrophy®
An Imprint of HarperCollins*Publishers*

HarperTrophy® is a registered trademark
of HarperCollins Publishers.

The Game of Silence
For information address HarperCollins Children's Books, a
division of HarperCollins Publishers, 10 East 53rd Street,
New York, NY 10022.
www.harperchildrens.com

Library of Congress Cataloging-in-Publication Data
Erdrich, Louise.
The game of silence / Louise Erdrich.— 1st ed.
p. cm.
Summary: Nine-year-old Omakayas, of the Ojibwa tribe,
moves West with her family in 1849.
ISBN-10: 0-06-441029-3 (pbk.)
ISBN-13: 978-0-06-441029-8 (pbk.)
1. Ojibwa Indians—Juvenile fiction. [1. Ojibwa Indians—
Fiction. 2. Indians of North America—Superior, Lake,
Region—Fiction. 3. Superior, Lake, Region—History—19th
century—Fiction.] I. Title.
PZ7.E72554Gam 2004   2004006018
[Fic]—dc22   CIP
                                                         AC

12 13 CG/BR 10 9 8 7 6
Typography by Amy Ryan
❖
First Harper Trophy edition, 2006

To Aza,
migiziins,
n'dawnis, gizhawenimin

CONTENTS

BIBOON (WINTER)

ZEEGWUN (SPRING)

PROLOGUE

Six black dots wavered on the far shore. Omakayas was the first to see them approach over the glittering waves, but there was no reason to call anyone yet. The sun was high, the wind against the travelers. There would be enough time. She was standing on her favorite rock, and she was thinking. Omakayas liked to arrange things in her mind. When she was deep in thought, she did not like to disturb herself, especially if her subject was as important as the order of all she loved.

The dots became the prows of canoes, jeemaanan. One by one, the tiny sticks of people and paddles appeared, heading right for Moningwanaykaning, her island, the

Island of the Golden-Breasted Woodpecker. She skipped a flat rock four skips, and then another four skips. Eight. One for each of those she loved the best. Carefully, Omakayas set their names into a design.

There was Andeg, her pet crow—black wings and a clever beak. Andeg was perched in a branch above the lakeshore, cleaning his feathers. He flew to her now, and landed on her shoulder. He knew she carried hazelnuts for him. Omakayas fed him a nut and kept thinking. There was Nokomis, her kind and accepting grandmother, the one who taught her to love plants and to use them as medicine. Next came Old Tallow! The thought of the old woman made her heart beat faster. Her love for the hunter Old Tallow was a fierce and tangled ball of feeling. As for her love for her brother, Pinch, it actually stung the roots of her hair. That was easy enough to feel! Pinch had pulled her braids only moments before, then run away. Underneath these loves was love for her older sister, Angeline, so beautiful and scarred, and of course her mother (even when she got mad) and her father (even when he was stern and distant). These loves were strong as earth. Last, there was the love loss of her tiniest brother, Neewo, who died two years ago, during the smallpox winter of 1847. That love was a deep black hole, bitter and profound.

She thought of these loves as she watched the six jeemaanan approach across the rough water. Andeg hopped down and plucked at her dress for another hazelnut. She took one from a small bag she kept at her waist, clenched it between her teeth, and smiled at Andeg. The crow knew the game and stretched his neck to delicately pluck the nut from Omakayas. She sat down to wait, then lay back in the sun and squinted at the jeemaanan. The party of canoes was battling a stiff wind offshore, but where she sat the air was calm.

Her name, Omakayas, meant Little Frog. She was nine winters old. On that rich early summer day, the jeemaanan approaching with possible excitement, anything seemed possible. The picture enlarged. She could now see  people of all ages in the jeemaanan, including children. Omakayas jumped up and stared hard. Her interest was stirred. So many people weren't coming just to visit family, and if they were coming to trade, there would be packs of skins visible. None were apparent. The presence of women and children meant that these people had left behind their camps and homes.

As they drew closer now, she saw the poorness of the canoes—some of them struggled to float. Behind the lead paddlers, the passengers bailed for their lives. No eagle feathers, beads, or red vermilion paint decorated the head men. There were no ribbons or beads on the clothing of the women—the poor rags barely covered them. Omakayas shouted. They were close enough now for her to see the expressions on their faces—open and pleading. She began to run and Andeg dived after her. Something was wrong. She didn't know what. It was a day she would think of long after as one in which her fate, and that of her family, took a great looping turn.

NEEBIN

SUMMER

ONE

THE RAGGEDY ONES

When they were close enough to touch bottom with their paddles, the people poured out of the nearly swamped canoes. The grown-ups held little ones and the little ones held even smaller ones. There were so many people jammed into each boat that it was a wonder they had made it across. The grown-ups, the ones who wore clothes, bunched around the young. A murmur of pity started among the people who had gathered on shore when they heard Omakayas's shout, for the children had no clothing at all, they were naked. In a bony, hungry, anxious group, the people from the boats waded ashore. They looked at the ground, fearfully and in shame. They were like skinny herons with long poles for legs and clothes like drooping feathers. Only their leader, a tall old man wearing a turban of worn cloth, walked with a proud step and held his head up as a leader should. He stood calmly, waiting for his people to assemble. When everyone was ashore and a crowd was gathered expectantly, he raised his thin hand and commanded silence with his eyes.

Everyone's attention was directed to him as he spoke.

"Brothers and sisters, we are glad to see you! Daga, please open your hearts to us! We have come from far away."

He hardly needed to urge kindness. Immediately, families greeted cousins, old friends, lost relatives, those they hadn't seen in years. Fishtail, a close friend of Omakayas's father, clasped the old chief in his arms. The dignified chief's name was Miskobines, Red Thunder, and he was Fishtail's uncle. Blankets were soon draping bare shoulders, and the pitiful naked children were covered, too, with all of the extra clothing that the people could find. Food was thrust into the hungry people's hands—strips of dried fish and bannock bread, maple sugar and fresh boiled meat. The raggedy visitors tried to contain their hunger, but most fell upon the food and ate wolfishly. One by one, family by family, the poor ones were taken to people's homes. In no time, the jeemaanan were pulled far up on the beach and the men were examining the frayed seams and fragile, torn stitching of spruce that held the birchbark to the cedar frames. Omakayas saw her grandmother, her sister, and her mother, each leading a child. Her mother's eyes were wide-set and staring with anger, and she muttered explosive words underneath her breath. That was only her way of showing how deeply she was affected; still, Omakayas steered clear. Her brother, Pinch, was followed by a tall skinny boy hastily wrapped in a blanket.

He was the son of the leader, Miskobines, and he was clearly struggling to look dignified. The boy looked back in exhaustion, as if wishing for a place to sit and rest. But seeing Omakayas, he flushed angrily and mustered strength to stagger on ahead. Omakayas turned her attention to a woman who trailed them all. One child clutched her ragged skirt. She carried another terribly thin child on a hip. In the other arm she clutched a baby. The tiny bundle in her arms made no movement and seemed limp, too weak to cry.

The memory of her poor baby brother, Neewo, shortened Omakayas's breath. She jumped after the two, leaving the intrigue of the story of their arrival for later, as well as the angry boy's troubling gaze. Eagerly, she approached the woman and asked if she could carry the baby.

The woman handed over the little bundle with a tired sigh. She was so poor that she did not have a cradle board for the baby, or a warm skin bag lined with rabbit fur and moss, or even a trade blanket or piece of cloth from the trader's store. For a covering, she had only a tiny piece of deerskin wrapped into a rough bag. Even Omakayas's dolls had better clothing and better care. Omakayas cuddled the small thing close. The baby inside the bag was bare and smelled like he needed a change of the cattail fluff that served as his diaper. Omakayas didn't mind. She carried the baby boy with a need and happiness that the woman, so relieved to hand the baby over, could not have guessed at. Having lost her own brother, Omakayas took comfort in this baby's tiny weight and light breath. She would protect him, she promised as they walked. She would keep him company and give him all the love she had stored up but could no longer give to her little brother Neewo.

The baby peered watchfully into her eyes. Though tiny and helpless, he seemed determined to live. With a sigh he rooted for milk, for something, anything. Anxiously, Omakayas hurried toward the camp.

The angry boy with the long stick legs and frowning face sat next to Pinch by the fire. He glared up when Omakayas entered the clearing, but then his whole attention returned to the bowl of stew in his hands. He stared into it, tense as an animal. He tried without success to keep from gulping the stew too fast. His hands shook so hard that he nearly dropped the bowl at one point, but with a furious groan he righted himself and attained a forced calm. Straining to control his hunger, he lifted the bowl to his lips and took a normal portion of meat between his teeth. Chewed. Closed his eyes. When Omakayas saw from beneath one half-shut eyelid the gleam of desperation, she looked away. Not fast enough.

"What are you staring at?" the boy growled.

"Nothing."

"Don't even bother with her," said Pinch, delighted to sense an ally with whom he might be able to torment his sister. "She's always staring at people. She's a homely owl!"

"Weweni gagigidoon," said Angeline, throwing an acorn that hit Pinch square on the forehead. She told her brother to speak with care, then commanded him, "Booni'aa, leave her alone!"

Omakayas was grateful to her big sister; still, she flushed and turned away. She was embarrassed by her brother's teasing, and also she felt it wrong to witness such hunger in the visitor. She could tell the boy was proud and it had hurt him to have his ravenous eating observed.

Besides that, she was, as usual, mad at Pinch. Sometimes the things he did were so awful that they instantly made her blood hot. At those times she had to run away before she hit him or screamed at him. Luckily, there were the other small children to occupy her immediately.

The scrawny little wide-eyed children dove into the food. They ate all they could and even licked one another's faces clean. When there was nothing in sight, they begged for more. At last, their bellies full, they fell asleep right where they sat, clutching some tattered old skins around them. That was when the woman, who ate politely and slowly, sighing with gratitude at each bite, spoke to Omakayas's mother, Yellow Kettle.

"This baby is not mine," she said. "We have been running for our lives. The Bwaanag wiped out our village. We left our gardens, our food caches, all of our kettles and our makazinan sitting by the doors. Some people even got left behind in the crazy mess. They were captured. That is why we have nothing. I don't know what happened to this baby's mother and father."

Omakayas's eyes filled with burning tears. She held the baby closer and let him go only when Mama, with a cooing lullaby and a cup of warm broth, took the baby to feed.

That was how Omakayas gained a brother that day, and a cousin, too, for the angry boy with bold eyes went to live at the camp that included her Auntie Muskrat and Uncle Albert LaPautre, as well as her girl cousins and her father's friend Fishtail.

From the first, the baby fascinated Omakayas. He was very different from Neewo and that was good, said Yellow Kettle, for the baby was his own little person. He had his very own spirit, and shouldn't be confused with the other. She, of course, never said the name of Neewo. Nobody said the names of those who had died. That was because to say their names would attract the spirits of the dead, even bring them back to visit the living. It was better to let even the most loved ones go along on their journey into the next world.

Anyway, this baby soon stopped reminding anyone of anybody but himself, for he was clever-eyed with a watchful face and a sharp bow of a mouth that he held in a quizzical line. Mama loved to hold him and sing to him while looking into his eyes. He needed to hear her baby songs, get used to her voice, she said. But Omakayas, whose arms ached to hold the baby too, understood that Mama needed to hold the new little one for her own healing. Mama even put this baby to her breast and let him nurse. After a while, she said, the baby would cause her body to remember how to make milk. When that happened, said Mama, with a gentle and confident look at the baby's pitiful legs and arms, the baby would rapidly grow fat. Nokomis quickly made the new baby a cradle board, bending a soaked piece of ash for the head guard and scraping a soft piece of fragrant cedar smooth for the back. Nokomis beaded two thick velvet bands to hold him against a soft cushion. As it was just the right time of year when the heads of the cattails explode into puffy sticks, Omakayas picked bags of cattail fluff to use as diapers. Once the baby was set inside the sack of the cradle board, he seemed to appreciate his new security and fell instantly asleep. But not for long. Whenever Omakayas turned around from her work, she'd see the baby watching her with such close attention that it seemed as though he was memorizing her every move. Nokomis gave him a nickname to match this sharp-eyed habit. She called him the little Bizheens, or baby wildcat, for the way the wild lynx stalks and watches its prey reminded her of the close and intent eyes of the baby.

One day, as Omakayas was watching Mama and Bizheens, she felt her Deydey watching her. He sat down next to her. Omakayas's Deydey was a prickly man— scratchy and remote sometimes, lost in his thoughts, or even cold as his name Mikwam, Ice. But he was also warmhearted and kind underneath. Often he seemed not to notice his surroundings at all as he worked on one of his many projects—nets, snowshoes, baskets, bows and arrows, traps . . . Deydey could make anything. Suddenly, he would lift his head from whatever he was doing and Omakayas would realize he had been closely observing the entire family all along. Now was one of those times.

"N'dawnis," he said, his hand warm on her hair, "don't be sad. Soon enough that little baby will be too much for your mama! She'll beg you to help her take care of him! And in the meantime," he went on, excitement in his voice, "I have made something for you."

Deydey put a small bundle into Omakayas's arms, folded her arms around the bundle, and hurried away. Giving gifts, the things he made, always embarrassed him. Omakayas recognized the scrap of hide, now cleaned and softened, that had first held Bizheens. Slowly, she pushed the edges away from a face that made her gasp. She saw beautiful hair, black bead eyes, and a tiny mouth reddened with vermilion. It was a wonderfully made doll with a dress of velvet sewed by Deydey and beaded by Omakayas's sister. Seeing Omakayas's longing, Deydey and Angeline had made her something to hold.

"I have a good family," Omakayas whispered. Holding the doll to her heart, she entered this precious being into the list of all she loved.

TWO

THE GAME OF SILENCE

Words. Words. Words. Pressing up from her stomach, trembling on her lips. Words buzzing in her throat like caught bees. Banging in her head. Harsh words. Angry words. Sounds boiling up in her like sap. Wild things she couldn't let out.

Yow! A kick from her brother almost caused Omakayas to blurt an exclamation.

No! Omakayas sealed her lips together in a firm line and glared at her brother with all of the force pent up inside. If the fire from her eyes could scorch him, Pinch would be the first to yell out. Then he would lose the game of silence. But Pinch was used to receiving furious looks from his family. He knew just how to respond. First he looked innocently at Omakayas (as though he was *ever* innocent!). He pretended he was unaware of the raging energy stuffed up inside of his sister. Then, as Omakayas bored her eyes at him with increasing intensity, he lolled out his tongue and twisted his face into a deranged and awful mask. His features shifted into one ugly and absurd face after the next until suddenly Omakayas just about . . . almost . . . laughed. Just in time, she clapped her hand to her mouth. Closed her eyes. Concentrated. Yes. Eya'. She would be a stone. Asineeg. A pile of stones. Each one harder and quieter than the next. She would be silent and more silent yet. And in spite of her annoying brother, she would win. She kept her eyes closed, put her forehead on her knees. Thought stone, stone, stone. Asin. Asin. Filled her mind with the sound of falling rain, which was easy. Outside, it was not just raining but *pouring* down a drenching, cold, miserable, early summer shower.

The rain had lasted for days, since the raggedy ones arrived. That was another thing. Besides Pinch, Omakayas couldn't stand rain anymore. The water made mush of tender new ground around her family's birchbark house. Droplets hissed through the roof vent into the fire, driving stinging smoke into her eyes. Everyone around her was affected. Nokomis's old bones ached and she creaked like a tree every time she moved. The watery wind sent coughs racking through her mother's chest. It was too wet to play outside, and cold when it should have been warm. Worst of all, Omakayas was stuck with Pinch.

He nudged her. Omakayas almost slugged him in return, but controlled herself. She'd had enough of him to last her whole life! She opened her eyes a fraction, then her eyes went wide in shock. Somehow, Pinch had got hold of her beloved doll, and he was making it teeter on the cliff of his knees. Omakayas bit her lip so hard it hurt. Pinch walked her doll to the edge of his knees, then teasingly back. If only Mama was here! If only she would return! Nokomis concentrated on her work so hard it was impossible to distract her.

Omakayas pretended to shut her eyes again, but cleverly watched until just the right moment to snatch back her doll. She sighed as though she was falling asleep and then, with a flash, she grabbed. Taken by surprise, Pinch couldn't react quickly enough to hold on, and Omakayas triumphantly clutched her doll. She stuck it down the neck of her dress. There! Safe! Inside, she laughed, but she didn't make a single sound, not a chirp, not so much as a mouse's squeak.

She was going to win the game of silence, she just knew it. Pinch was now poking little twigs into the fire in the center fire pit, watching them burn. Omakayas tried not to notice him, but his head was so big and fuzzy. Pinch's hair sprang out with its own energy. Crafty eyes in his tough, round face calculated his sister's endurance. He was surely cooking up some mischief. Sure enough, Pinch drew the burning wand from the fire and laid it innocently next to her ankle—as though she didn't know that it would scorch her if she moved the slightest inch! And make her cry out, first, and instantly lose the game! She kicked it back at him.

"Gego, Pinch," she nearly warned, but bit her lip.

"Eah, eah, eah," he mouthed the taunt, making an impossibly irritating face that almost broke Omakayas's discipline.

Luckily, just at the second that Omakayas decided to forfeit the game and to smash her little brother over the head with the big tin soup ladle, the visitors arrived.

"They are here," said their grandmother. "You can quit the game until after we eat."

"Aaaagh!" Omakayas exploded with such a wild sound of rage that Nokomis jumped. Pinch retreated, unnerved by how sorely he'd tested his sister. Omakayas breathed out in relief. These visitors were her friends and cousins—Twilight, Little Bee, and Two Strike Girl. They had brought the boy she called, in her mind, the Angry One. Her cousins were her favorite friends, the ones she counted on. Twilight was much like her name, quiet and thoughtful. Little Bee was funny and bold. Two Strike was tough and she could do anything a boy could do, usually better. Since her mother had died, she was wilder than ever. Even her father had not been able to handle Two Strike, and had left her with Auntie Muskrat. But Auntie Muskrat had had no success in taming Two Strike. Sometimes she was so fierce that she outdid everyone—it was a challenge to play with her. The girls had learned to sew and bead together, gathered berries, and helped their mothers clean fish. They also learned early on how to tan hides, a task that Omakayas despised. And now too, her sister, Angeline, was home. Omakayas grinned with satisfaction. Pinch was delightfully outnumbered by girls and would pout, creeping to Mama's side when she arrived, and turning into a baby, hoping to be pampered with tidbits of meat and maple sugar.

Now everyone—the children and their parents—squeezed into the lodge. They had made the lodge extra big that summer, for visitors. For the first time, it was

packed entirely full, but there was enough room for everyone. Even the Angry One found a space to sit. He glared
from a little spot against the wall. Together, they ate rich
venison soup from the shallow birchbark makakoon they'd
brought along with them. Two other men squeezed in,
important men. Old Tallow entered, huge and rangy and
smelling of wolf. She settled herself while outside her ferocious dogs stood guard, unmoving and alert even in the
pelting rain. Each of Old Tallow's feet seemed to take up
as much space as a small child, but Omakayas didn't mind.
Warily, but completely, she loved the fierce old woman.

Each visitor brought a gift for the pile that the children
who won the game of silence would choose from that
night. For it was an important night. With the raggedy
ones came serious doings. Difficult questions and impossible news. Great attention was needed. The grown-ups
needed to council, think, absorb the facts, without having
to shush small children. The children could tell how
important the meeting was from the degree to which their
silence was required. The pile of treats was the best ever.

There was a bag of marbles, some of actual glass, not
just clay. A pair of narrow makazinan that Omakayas
thought just might fit her. One doll, elaborately dressed in
a tiny set of britches and a leather coat. A sharp knife. A
deer knuckle game. Two duck's bills of maple sugar tied
together with split jack-pine root. Six red ribbons. A little
roll of flowered cloth. Eight tiny bells. One small bow, and

six arrows tipped with real brass points cut from a trade kettle. The arrows were fletched with the sharp black and yellow feathers of a bird that the island where they lived was named for—the golden-breasted woodpecker. Old Tallow must have brought them. What treasures! The children examined them breathlessly, each picking out one particular prize they meant to win.

Little Bee, of course, wanted the doll. Two Strike Girl, the bow and arrows. Pinch coveted the knife, but he was torn by greed for the maple sugar and the need for marbles to replace those he'd lost. The Angry One did not deign to move from his spot or look at the gifts. No doubt he'd have no problem winning the game! As for Twilight, quiet and serene, she had no trouble playing the game and she would be content with anything. Omakayas wanted the ribbons, the bells, and the marbles, too, but she settled on the makazinan because she had watched her grandmother make them so carefully. They were fancy, with velvet ankle cuffs, the tops beaded with flowers and little white sparkling vines. Worth her silence!

Now the grown-ups were ready to start talking. Nokomis sang the song of the game of silence four times, nearly catching Pinch at the end. Then she turned away from them too, absorbed in the talk.

Omakayas looked longingly at Twilight, and her cousin made a sad and frustrated face. With her favorite cousin so close and her annoying brother so near, it was difficult to play. If only they could talk! At first, the girls communicated by mouthing words and moving their eyes, but the temptation to laugh was too great. They turned away from each other unwillingly. Omakayas listened to the rain, a solid drumming and hissing. Then she listened to the fire crackling and sighing. She watched the beautiful and changing glow of the coals. At some point, Omakayas couldn't tell exactly when, her attention was caught by something her father said. And then she noticed that her cousin Twilight was also listening to the grownups' conversation. Soon, they all couldn't help but listen. They leaned forward, straining to hear every sound, almost forgetting to breathe.

That night, for the first time, everybody got their prizes. Nobody lost the game of silence. For that night they knew the threat of a much bigger loss. They would all fear to lose something huge, something so important that they never even knew that they had it in the first place. Who questions the earth, the ground beneath your feet? They had always accepted it—always here, always solid.

That something was home.

Omakayas's father, Mikwam, touched his heart and spoke with a troubled frown.

"We do not use the black marks of the chimookomanag," he said, "because we keep the record here."

The chimookomanag were the white people. The black marks that Mikwam spoke of were the writing that Angeline learned day by day at the mission school in the town of LaPointe. The writing was very strange to Omakayas. Black marks that captured sounds. Tracks across paper or slate boards or birchbark that stood for words spoken. How did the odd scratching connect to the sounds? All a mysterious business, and one that her father, anyway, did not trust.

The Ojibwe relied on memory. They repeated stories, songs, the words to promises and treaties. Everyone memorized all that was important. Although people scratched elaborate signs on birchbark and rolled them into scrolls, they relied on memory to go with the marks. Memory was Ojibwe writing. Things were not forgotten that way. Something about the black marks had gone wrong, Omakayas knew that. The black marks promised one thing, but the chimookomanag wanted to break that promise.

"We signed a paper that said they could take the trees. We signed a paper that said they could take the copper *from* the earth," said the old chief Bizhiki, disturbed, "we didn't say they could take the earth."

"Who can take the earth?"

Fishtail spoke, gesturing with his strong and eloquent

hands. He was a young man, he expressed his opinions well. The whole family liked Fishtail, but Angeline liked him the best of all. She watched him shyly from beneath her long eyelashes. "I'll tell you," he answered himself, turning just a little toward Angeline as though she gave off a warming glow, "when the chimookomanag open up the earth they believe they own it just like a kettle, just like this deerskin, just like this knife!"

The other men laughed, and the women put their hands to their faces, but it was a bitter laughter because everyone knew what he said was true. Here is what had happened. The ogimaa or the president of all of the chimookomanag had sent a message to the leaders of the Ojibwe. That message was simple. They must leave their homes. The ogimaa said that the government now owned the ground they lived on. It was needed for white settlers. He had issued a removal order. He had decided that land payments would be given out in a new place in the west.

But the western land was the home of the Bwaanag. The raggedy ones had tried to live there and look what had happened.

"There was a time when we had no quarrel with the Bwaanag," said Deydey. "They lived in their part of the world and we in ours. We even traded with them. But as the chimookamanag push us, so we push the Bwaanag. We are caught between two packs of wolves."

"We can't go to the west," cried Albert LaPautre.

LaPautre was comical, chubby, and sometimes cowardly. "Our enemies will kill us with knives," he cried. "They will shoot our brains out, club us in the kidneys, raise our scalps, burn us, cut us into little pieces—"

"Saaah!" Nokomis silenced him. "You're scaring yourself!"

The children were riveted, staring in horror, each imagining some dreadful death. Pinch's eyes were the biggest, round as two moons. Although he acted tough and always shouted fiercely when playing at imaginary battles, he was still a little boy. Now he crept closer to Yellow Kettle and bent his frowzy head to lean against her. Omakayas saw that he had taken a corner of Mama's skirt between his fingers, and he clung to it for reassurance.

"Still, we must be brave," said LaPautre. "The chimookomanag owe us payment for the land they took. I intend to collect." He folded his arms over his round pumpkin of a stomach and tried to look determined and fearless.

"Here is what I think," said a man named Cloud, "we have done something to offend. One or two of our hot-hearted brothers must have killed a chimookoman!"

"Eya', geget," said Mikwam slowly, "that is possible."

Old Tallow reared herself up in the light. She wore her hat with the feather even in the lodge. Now she spoke in the abrupt snarl of a person used to giving, not ever taking, orders.

"Perhaps we have broken our promise to be peaceful and treat them kindly! Send runners out. Send out michitweg. Find what our foolish brothers have done. Then we can punish the wrongdoers and stay here. *Right here.*"

Beneath her words, there was a desperation that Omakayas had never heard before in Old Tallow's tough growl. The powerful woman was attached to her cabin, to her hunting territory, to the level patch of sand and the canopy where she and Omakayas's father constructed expertly balanced and seamless jeemaanan of the perfect bark found on this island. Old Tallow had never traveled far from her home in her life, and she was unwilling to start now.

Another friend of Mikwam, the wise leader Buffalo, agreed that it was a good idea to find out who was responsible for the chimookomanag change of heart. "Who will go?" he asked.

Cloud answered that he would scout to the south. A swift young man said he would travel to the east. Fishtail said that he would travel to the west and yet another man accepted the responsibility of the north. They would meet at a place called Sandy Lake and then return to the island in one year. It was no surprise that Fishtail would leave, for two winters ago he had lost his beloved wife.

"After all, I have nothing . . . ," he began, by way of explaining his willingness to go on this dangerous mission. He was going to say that he had no reason to stay on the island. But suddenly he stopped. His brow creased and he turned his head just a fraction, gazing with a surprised tenderness at the lovely, scarred face of Angeline. There was a long beat of silence between Angeline and Fishtail, though they were not playing the children's game.

Perhaps, Omakayas thought later, when she understood the messages between the two that night, Fishtail might have stayed that year if only Angeline had made some gesture. But Angeline was too shy and uncertain to look at him. By the time she was able to meet his glance, he had committed himself to go on the dangerous journey into the land of the Bwaanag. Albert would take other men, too, and investigate the promise of payments far off, near a place called Sandy Lake.

"I'll go too!"

Two Strike Girl jumped to her feet with a loud cry, then clapped her hand over her mouth. But she was forgiven her outburst by the men, by the kind leader Buffalo, and by Mikwam and by Omakayas's grandmother.

"Howah! Brave-hearted girl!" said Fishtail, smiling, and Two Strike Girl sat down again, proud of the fire in her heart, wishing that she could fight. Omakayas couldn't help noticing that the Angry One looked at Two Strike with a combination of emotions—annoyance? admiration? Did he want to shout at Two Strike or did he want to fight alongside her? He caught Omakayas looking at him suddenly and looked down. His face was angrier than ever, but he also looked confused.

The morning that the men left was ordinary, sunny, and calm. Yellow Kettle and Angeline packed dried meat, dried fish, a pair of leggings, and some tobacco for Fishtail. The girls walked down to the dock from which each of the jeemaanan would embark. The other men were already gone. Fishtail was the last. There he stood, patiently. It looked like he was waiting. Maybe, thought Omakayas, someone else was coming. He was staring so intently in their direction that Omakayas looked behind them. But no, he was staring at Angeline.

The two girls approached, and then, as they arrived,

Omakayas couldn't help but notice that her sister's hand trembled as she gave the package of traveling provisions to Fishtail. Omakayas watched him intently when he took the pack from Angeline, to see if his eyes would soften. Sure enough, she thought that she detected a certain question in his gaze.

She kept watching him, and then realized that both he and her sister were staring right at her.

"Geewen," ordered Angeline in a sharp voice. "Go home."

Omakayas felt an instant pang of hurt and surprise. Her sister, so beautiful, hurt her feelings sometimes. Not as often now as she had before she'd suffered the sickness that scarred her cheeks, but often enough. Now was one of those times. Omakayas couldn't hide her shame. She glanced at Fishtail to say good-bye, but then saw that his eyes warmly praised her. He smiled his thanks.

"Meegwech, little one," he said, then bent near to look straight into her eyes. He was not afraid, as some young men are, to be kind. At that moment, Omakayas loved him very much. "I will remember you when I'm far away in the land of the Bwaanag. Don't be sad. I'll return by the time the earth warms again. And now, my little sister, will you leave me alone with your big sister for a moment? I must say good-bye to her too."

"You can say good-bye to her right now," said Omakayas. Stubborn, she held her ground. Fishtail smiled and shook his head so understandingly, however, that she couldn't refuse. For a moment, before she left, he held her around the shoulders. She ran off smiling, proud that he was her friend. Then she slowed to a walk, and her heart thudded. Fishtail's travels would last until next year.

By the time the earth warms again.

Omakayas sat at some distance and watched her sister take leave of Fishtail. Nothing special happened, they just talked. Then Fishtail got into the center of the jeemaan and lifted his paddle. With a broad, smooth movement he was launched far past the dock. Once the jeemaan was no more than a black smudge, tiny and almost invisible between the dark of the water and the trees of the far shore, Omakayas became restless. She tapped her toes in the sand, jumped up, sat down, waited, called her sister once or twice. But Angeline did not answer, nor did she move. Angeline continued to stand onshore watching the place where Fishtail had disappeared.

After the men had left, the camps were very quiet. Sounds seemed louder. There was leftover stew in pots, and too much room in the lodges. Angeline was short of temper or too silent. Even Deydey, missing his good friend, Fishtail, brooded. Every night he sat at the fire and stared into the flames without speaking or even making anything. To see his hands idle was strange. Maybe he wished he'd gone along to share the hardships and dangers. Maybe he was planning something that required much thought. It was a relief to Omakayas to get away, even if it meant sharing work with Nokomis.

Every morning, Omakayas and Andeg visited Grandmother's garden and helped the plants along. Deydey had found a piece of tough root-wood, and from it he'd fashioned a perfectly balanced short digging tool for Omakayas. A gnarled handle made it easy to grip and the end, filed flat and sharpened, was good for chopping weeds. The sun beat down on Omakayas. First her hair turned hot, then her shoulders. Sweat seeped down the sides of her face and ran along her collarbone. Her eyes stung with salt and her arms ached. She was glad for Andeg's company. As she worked, he walked beside her or hopped in flapping bounds to peck up grubs and worms and beetles that her hoe unearthed. Sometimes he flew a short way off into the woods and Omakayas heard him talking to other crows. But he always returned to her. His calls sounded like encouragement. Yah! Yah!

Nokomis's garden was very old. She had inherited it from her mother, who had inherited it from hers. The earth had grown rich from generations of careful replenishment. All around the edges of the garden a stout fence of driftwood, hung with cheerful rags of clothing, protected the earth and the tender plants. But the garden was more than the space it occupied. Its seeds, too, had been handed down for many generations. During the worst of the family's hunger, two winters ago, Nokomis had finally insisted that they eat half of her seed beans, but only because she'd saved extra. Nobody even thought of eating more. Nokomis's seeds, after all, were the future. While Nokomis piled beach weeds around the new shoots of beans and muttered to herself or the plants, Omakayas was never sure which, Andeg made a game of perching on one driftwood fence pole and then the next, as though trying each one out. Some made him critical. From others, he cawed joyfully. Everything felt so right and familiar to Omakayas that the sudden thought that they could be removed from their home was a crash of impossibility.

"They can't send us away, can they?" she asked Nokomis as they helped the pumpkin vines twine toward the stalks of corn, which would shortly be tall. "They can't do anything, really, Nokomis, can they? There are so few chimookamanag and so many of us!"

Nokomis leaned back, kneeling in the dirt. Omakayas was surprised that she had stopped her work. Almost nothing got Nokomis to stop once she started on her garden. But now her face was serious.

"Listen, my little one," she said, "for I'm going to tell you the truth. The chimookomanag we see here are only the first drops of rain. A storm of them lives past the sunrise, in the east. They can flood us like a river."

"Can't we stop them?"

"We have seen what happens to others when they

resist, go to war. The river wipes them out. Our way is different. We have always found out how to live with them, work with them, trade with them, even to marry them!"

Nokomis's eyes fixed on Omakayas with amusement and Omakayas smiled back. Deydey's grandfather had been a French trader, one of the first. Deydey had grown up in a house made of trees, like the cabin he'd built for his family. This alone marked him out as different.

"I think Deydey is figuring out a plan," said Omakayas. "He is always staring at the fire, thinking hard."

"I hope you're right," Nokomis said. Her look rested tenderly upon her granddaughter. "This is a good place, and I hoped for you to grow up here and become a strong woman."

"I love it here so much," Omakayas admitted. Suddenly her eyes grew hot, her chest tight. "It is where my little brother rests."

Nokomis patted her hand and smoothed Omakayas's hair back with gentle fingers. Omakayas leaned into her grandmother's arms and for a long time the two sat in the garden, on the sun-warmed earth, listening to the birds call and talk to one another unseen in the dense green of the woods. If they ever had to leave, Omakayas felt, her heart might fall right out of her body to lie forever on the ground it loved.

THREE

FISH SOUP

Mama and Nokomis were weaving reed pukwe mats outside in the shade of a maple tree. They used long flat matting needles that Deydey fashioned of bone. As he did with everything that he made for his beloved wife and her mother, the needles were extra special, decorated with circles and crosses. The matting needles and the reeds ticked and rustled together, and the sitting mats grew bigger and bigger. While the two women worked, the new little baby, Bizheens, watched each mat develop under their hands. The women laughed, for his baby gaze was as critical and solemn as an old man's. Just as Mama predicted, he was growing plumper so quickly that he seemed rounder every morning, as though he was adding baby fat in his sleep. They touched his nose, jiggled the tiny dream catcher that dangled just over his forehead. His cradle board hung off a low branch and from time to time Nokomis swung him lightly. When she did, his eyes sparked with alarm first, then pleasure, and he made a sharp little cooing sound of happy surprise. Still, he never laughed.

"Can I go to Auntie Muskrat's?" Omakayas asked.

Even though the Angry Boy was living at Auntie Muskrat's, Omakayas decided to risk his burning glare in order to play with her cousins.

"Go ahead," said Mama, "you helped me a lot today."

With a grateful shout, Omakayas shot off down the path. Andeg swooped out of the tree where he had perched, waiting, and followed her down the trail. All the way to her cousins' house, Pinch followed her, too. He stayed just out of sight, making the sounds of bear grunts as though he thought she would be afraid. Sometimes he threw a small stick at her or ran ahead beside the path, hidden by woods, to see if he could ambush her. But always Andeg found him out and gave a harsh, mocking call that sounded just like a laugh. From all her years of living with her brother, Omakayas was used to this. In her hand, she carried a long thin stick of whiplike green wood. When Pinch tried to creep up behind her to frighten her,

Omakayas, listening to Andeg, turned at the exact right moment and gave him a whack with the stick. She did so without thinking, by reflex.

Whack! Absentmindedly, she thumped the stick about an inch from her brother's head.

"Missed me!" he cried, trying to mock her but a little warier. She'd come very close!

Omakayas swung again. Life as an older sister wasn't easy. A brother like Pinch made it especially hard. Luckily, she had Andeg. And Twilight also understood her situation perfectly, for she had to handle a sister, Little Bee, who seemed to have a special way of doing just the right thing to drive her crazy. And both Omakayas and Twilight also had to contend with their cousin Two Strike Girl, who was difficult and even explosive.

Just now, as they turned into the camp where Auntie Muskrat and her husband, Albert LaPautre, lived, Omakayas sniffed the air and suddenly knew what was coming. A fishy fresh soup smell greeted her, that was the good part. The not-so-good part was the more powerful smell of raw fish blood. The nets had been unloaded. A big catch had just come in and there was work to do. The fish must be gutted, cut apart, and dried in the sun. Even now, Twilight, Two Strike, Little Bee, and the angry new boy cousin were using spruce-root fibers to tie twigs together into fish-drying racks.

"Just in time!" Auntie Muskrat waggled her sharp knife at Omakayas, who looked around to find, of course, that Pinch had disappeared at the first sign of work. Little Bee carried the doll she had won in a little backpack tikinagun. Omakayas saw that Twilight had sewn her ribbons carefully onto the straps of her dress. They fluttered a bit, the tails touching the tops of her arms. Twilight was very neat, and careful to keep the satin of her ribbons away from the fishy work. She calmly smiled, nodded at her cousin as she approached, and proceeded to expertly slice each fish down the underside of its belly. After she gutted the fish she tossed it to her mother, who then boned it with a thin knife so sharp that their uncle used it, each morning, to shave the twenty-three hairs off his chin.

Omakayas tried to contain her dismay. She gulped, sighed. There was a big pile of fish at her elbow. She'd managed to evade one set of chores only to find herself trapped at the very place where so often she found freedom. But, as Omakayas had a practical nature and the soup smelled delicious and was thick with little blue-skinned potatoes from Auntie Muskrat's garden, she shrugged and set to work. She took her knife out of its sheath on her belt. The sheath was beautifully beaded, a gift from Nokomis. Omakayas slit open a fish as long as her arm and plunged her hands into the slippery fish guts.

"Meegwech, Nimisay," said Twilight gratefully, calling her sister, "the sooner we finish, the sooner we can go play at our place!"

Two Strike, who liked anything to do with knives, jumped to the task eagerly. She was strong, her muscles were hard ropes. Her face was stubborn-chinned with a sensitive mouth. All around them, dogs from the village soon gathered. Whenever there was fish or meat to be cut up, dogs appeared instantly, as though a mysterious call went out all over the island. One dignified black dog belonging to Old Tallow even stalked in to sit companionably just outside the circle. The dogs watched every tiny movement of the girls' hands, their eyes fixed and focused. From above, Andeg also waited. As soon as a hand paused to flip a fish scrap to the side, a mouth was there to catch it and bolt it down with a doggy gulp, or Andeg darted down to snatch it on the wing. The girls worked swiftly. Every time a hand moved, there was an almost simultaneous snap from dog teeth. Omakayas, of course, tossed the best scraps to her crow. Twilight had a favorite dog, a spotted one who must have had a chi-mookoman missionary's dog for a father. This puppy was not light-boned and thin, with long wolf legs like the other dogs in camp. He was heavier and a little odd, with one ear that stuck up and one that flopped down, and a strange mottled coat of black and red and even a little white. Twilight made sure that her favorite dog got plenty of scraps, while Omakayas and Two Strike, who liked them all the same, were careful to feed each one in turn.

With all of them working, the pile of fish was soon done. Auntie Muskrat, with a comfortable swish of her wood ladle, dipped out makakoon of fish soup. Then she wiped her knife clean on a leaf and sliced off long thick pieces of that morning's bannock. They dunked the bread in the soup and used the tough bread for spoons. With the softened bannock they polished up the last bits of soup. At last, Auntie Muskrat gave them each a special treat and sprinkled a pinch of salt carefully along each stick of soup-softened bannock. They slowly ate each bite, lingering over the salty goodness.

THE MUD PEOPLE

After they were finished eating, the cousins left to set up their play camp. They had made a clearing next to a fascinating slough filled with swampy thick water, mud for frogs and turtles, tiny fish for herons, and lots of weedy shallows for ducks. Usually, when the air was still, the place swarmed with mosquitoes. But as there was a breeze today, there were only a few to bother them. A great gnarled willow reared up near the water, its shape excitingly monstrous. The tree looked like a big creature crawling up the bank, leaving one trailing tail-root to suck up water. Omakayas and Twilight prepared their camp around the base of the tree, while Little Bee helped. Two Strike made her home in the tree itself, where she could scout for enemies. She was in the tree now. Suddenly Two Strike shouted that she saw the imaginary approach of Bwaanag warriors who were really leaves and squirrels.

"If you shout like that," said Twilight, standing at the base of the tree, "the enemies will know just where you are. Better to climb down, whisper in my ear, then go bash them dead."

Two Strike scowled, knowing that her cousin had a good point. She was as irritated with her cousins for being sensible as they were irritated with her for having a loud and ferocious nature. Her behavior included what Twilight called those "Two Strike ways"—yelling loudly and jerking things out of people's hands and rushing impatiently here and there to fix things or hunt things down. Twilight had her own ways, though, of dealing with her cousin.

"We do need a strong warrior scout right now," she said in her most convincing voice, "someone to watch for two warriors who will try to sneak up on us. One will probably look like Pinch, the other might look like that angry stranger Mama let into our house. Don't be fooled, they are enemies! Tell us when you see them!"

Omakayas looked at her cousin in admiration. With one suggestion, she had satisfied Two Strike by giving her just the important job she liked, plus they would now have warning when the boys approached. Also, with Two Strike on their side instead of against them, they could surely prevent the boys from trampling their camp, knocking over their pine bough shelters, spilling their water, stealing their mats, and kidnapping their children.

Their boys and girls were made out of reeds and corn husks. They slept on tiny mats near the fire and ate stick-mud stew from off flat rocks. The children had a great many toys made of little pebbles, and they used acorn-cap bowls and leaves for dishes. With Two Strike watching over them, they worked at their play with great attention. They took care of each child in turn, then set up a small lodge using thin poles and some old discarded bark from the edge of the summer camp.

"Let's pretend it's night and we have to go inside," said Omakayas, admiring the little lodge.

It looked so cozy that she wanted to crawl inside, but it was small. The three girls squeezed in, then reached out and dragged their children in along with them, and closed the door. The hut was so small that they could barely take a breath, but they sat inside anyway, proud of what they'd done. Carefully, making only the smallest of cramped movements, they put their husk and reed children to bed. The girls smoothed down the leaf bedcovers and sang lullabies, gently smoothing back their children's invisible hair. They touched their babies' invisible noses, kissed their mouths and cheeks.

Wham! As though a tornado slammed into the hut, the girls went tumbling every which way. The bark covering flew off, bounced, and rolled into the slough. The carefully constructed roof floated into a clump of weeds. Twilight tumbled one way and Omakayas the other. Their reed children scattered in pieces and all of their dishes and foods were tossed in a wild heap. Even before she saw him, Omakayas knew that Pinch was the burst of bad weather that destroyed their play world. She bounded to her feet, determined to punish him, but he'd made his quick, destructive raid and then disappeared.

"Where'd he go?" cried Little Bee. Two Strike Girl

jumped out of the tree with a hideous yell, to defend her cousins, but tripped on the trees roots and sprawled flat. She hadn't seen Pinch vanish. Narrowing her eyes, she controlled herself. Stamping her feet, she called with a menacing pleasantness in her voice. "Piiinch, Piiinch, come on back so we can play. I just want to play with you, Piiinch!"

There was no answer and Pinch was not fooled.

Only because she happened to glance up did Omakayas notice that Pinch had clambered up the hunched willow tree and was now trying to stay hidden, flattened out on a high branch that hung above the water. Shushing her cousin, she pointed out Pinch's whereabouts to Two Strike, whose eyes lighted with vengeful pleasure.

"Wait here, pretend you don't see him," said Two Strike Girl. "I have an idea."

With that, she ran off to Auntie Muskrat's. Omakayas looked at Twilight, who whispered to Little Bee. They shrugged and decided to play along. They wailed and wrung their hands beneath the tree. Above them, Pinch, filling with huge satisfaction at the success of his attack, kept quiet and listened with delight to their voices.

"It was a warrior," cried Twilight.

"Powerful!" Omakayas agreed loudly, adding in a whisper, "We'll make him sorry when he comes down!"

They continued to lament, while Pinch swelled with satisfaction. Two Strike Girl returned. Sneaking around the base of the tree, she launched herself into the branches. She was carrying something. Omakayas and Twilight crept below to look and saw that she was steadily climbing toward Pinch. They started with horror. Between her teeth, her mouth stretched wide to hold the weapon, she carried her uncle's hatchet!

"Noooo!" Twilight screamed at the sight of her cousin, advancing murderously toward Pinch.

"Gego! Gego!" Omakayas ran to the tree, sure that Two Strike meant to use the hatchet on her brother. No matter how awful he was, she couldn't let anything happen to him. But Two Strike had different intentions. When she reached the branch upon which her cousin was hiding, she stopped near the base. Pinch, his eye on the hatchet, inched backward in fright. His mouth dropped open as, with strong, sure strokes, Two Strike began to chop.

She did not stop for Pinch's pleading. She did not stop for her sister's laughter. She did not stop to mock Pinch. She concentrated on her chopping. Whenever Pinch plucked up the courage to edge toward her, she brandished the hatchet with such a horrible growl that he cringed in fear. She kept chopping, chopping, until at last, with a great crack, the branch gave and Pinch toppled off the leafy end into the green slough mud below.

He did not splash. The slimy ooze simply gulped him in. When he came up, and with a great yell of outrage began to stalk out of the muck, the girls were overcome with laughter. He dripped absurdly, tufts of stinking weed sprouting off his shoulders and hair.

"Hiyn!" Pinch grabbed the one closest to him, Twilight, wrestled her quickly to the edge of the wet grime, and shoved her into the muck. He ran back for Two Strike and Little Bee. Omakayas yelled but stayed just out of her brother's reach. Fueled by muddy rage, he was irresistibly strong and quick. He managed to get into a clinch with Two Strike Girl, a hold so fierce that neither of them could break it. Suddenly, from behind a screen of leaves, the angry boy jumped. Before Omakayas could drag Pinch away or help Twilight and Little Bee from the mess, he had grabbed the kicking, scratching, screaming Two Strike Girl. Together, the boys carried her to the edge and dumped her into the mud, which had gathered a rich mold on top. In she went! Twilight dragged Pinch back in with her. Suddenly there was only Omakayas and the angry boy, the two of them face-to-face.

"Oh, it's you again," said the boy.

He didn't say it in a mean way, but he looked at her with those raging eyes and before she knew it Omakayas surprised herself. She grabbed him by the shoulders. Taken off guard, he stepped backward. Then he pushed back. They were both strong, and there is no telling who would have pushed who in first had not the ones from the slough, now completely doused with mud, jumped out and pushed the two clean ones before them, sending them flying farthest of all with one great heave.

When they were all covered with the stinking mud, throwing sloppy handfuls, roiling up the sticky shore, it occurred to them that Auntie Muskrat, not to mention Yellow Kettle, would not exactly be pleased to see them when they returned home. So the mud people made their way down a path to the waters of the huge, clean lake. There, they ducked and swam until the mud was thoroughly cleaned out of their clothing. Then they chose flat sunny rocks and lay down to dry themselves. As they did so the boy, whose anger was doused with the ridiculous mud, sat quietly next to Omakayas. He sat there so long that she finally began to talk to him.

"Do you like it over there at Auntie Muskrat's?" asked Omakayas.

The boy shrugged and looked very hard at the rock, and she didn't press him for an answer. He gave one anyway, though it took a long time.

"It's good. I guess I . . . ," he gulped. "I miss my old home. Too many got sick back there," he said. "My mother got sick. Then the Bwaanag . . ." his voice trailed off in sorrow. "But I do like it here. I want to stay in this place. I don't want to go anywhere, ever again!"

Omakayas nodded in understanding now and surprised herself by grabbing a rock and bashing it at the waves. She was mad at the ogimaa who sent Fishtail off to the west. She was furious at how her family was told to leave their island. The Angry One looked at her in surprise, then took a rock too, slammed it hard at the water.

"My father says we never had these kinds of problems," he said, "until the long knives, the chimookomanag, came among us."

"Geget sa."

Omakayas knew that very well. Chimookomanag. They were the source of some nice things like kettles and warm blankets and ribbons, and the source of terrible things, too. Chimookomanag brought sickness. Her grandmother's medicines were useless when chimookomanag diseases struck. Chimookomanag illness needed chimookoman medicine. From her own sudden furious reaction, too, she suddenly understood the fury of the Angry One. The pain of losing her tiny brother to the spotted illness would always be in her heart. Anger was a way not to give in to a great sadness. Omakayas wanted to show the Angry One that she understood, but didn't know how, so she just gave him another rock to smash at nothing.

"Let's go back," said the boy after a while, "maybe your Auntie has some more of that soup." He was hungry, always hungry. He still could never get enough. He'd starved so badly on the long and desperate journey to this island that he would never be completely full.

THE BREAK-APART GIRL

Among the good things that the chimookamanag had brought, there was a chimookoman girl. Omakayas and Twilight had made friends with her. They called her the Break-Apart Girl. The next day they decided to visit her. She lived near town. They walked to the cabin of cut boards where she lived, and as they approached they heard the music she made on the great toothed box that she called a piano. The tinkling notes were sweet and light. They seemed to shimmer on the breeze. Omakayas and Twilight stood close to the house looking at the windows and doors. Soon the girl herself appeared in a window and waved. Then she came out of the house and walked toward them, smiling, holding her skirt like a basket. As always, they saw that her dress nearly cut her in half. Her waist was so tiny that it always looked as though she was ready to snap. That was why they had named her the Break-Apart Girl.

Not only did the girl's dress look painful, but her hard shiny shoes, buttoned up the sides, made arrows of her feet and were useless for running. Omakayas pitied her. The chimookoman girl couldn't run and could hardly breathe. Today, though, her face was eager. In her skirt, they saw, she carried great red fruits. Carefully, the Break-Apart Girl gave some of the fruits to Omakayas, and others to Twilight. The last few, she kept to herself. Nodding at the girls, she opened her mouth. Her teeth were rather small and weak-looking, still, she took a great snapping bite from the apple. The cousins did the same, and then the three walked along to the shore of the lake. There, they sat on rocks, eating the fragrant apples very slowly, catching up the apple juice that dribbled down their chins.

Omakayas was the first to remove her makazinan. She took her shoes off and ran her feet through the warm sand. Twilight was next. With a look of excited intrigue, the Break-Apart Girl decided to take her shoes off too. It took a long time to undo all of the buttons, but at last her feet were bare. The sight of the Break-Apart Girl's bare feet startled Omakayas, for the girl's feet were strangely shaped, the toes gnarled together and pointed, and all of them a dead white unhealthy-looking color. Her feet were, Omakayas was ashamed to think it, ugly. Now she knew why the mission women and the Break-Apart Girl always wore their feet covered, so carefully buttoned up in strong leather. Their feet looked terrible. Omakayas felt pity once more and looked away, over the dark blue waves. Soon the Break-Apart Girl was doing as Omakayas was, running her feet in and out of the sun-warmed sand. The girls decided, pointing and laughing, to test the water.

Omakayas and Twilight hoisted their dresses, and so did the Break-Apart Girl. Then, Omakayas envied her a little. Underneath the drab color of her dress, she wore a big ruffed skirt of shiny fabric, striped red and white just like sticks of trader's candy. It was very beautiful, and Omakayas kept trying not to stare. The girls ran into the water. Then they pranced back up the beach and buried their feet, once again, in the warm sand.

47

After they all put their shoes back on, Omakayas pointed at herself.

"Omakayas," she said.

"Omayukya," said the Break-Apart Girl.

They all laughed. They had tried this before, and knew that they couldn't say one another's names.

"Clarissa," the girl said, touching her chest.

"Gisina," said Omakayas, and Twilight laughed because it was the word people said when they walked outdoors in winter and the icy wind blasted them. Gisina! It's sure cold! When the light hit the Break-Apart Girl's blue eyes, Omakayas shivered a little, for she could not get used to their ghostly color.

Omakayas pointed back toward the house full of what the Ojibweg called slave animals, the awakaanag, that lived out back of the Break-Apart Girl's house. They went to visit these odd creatures. The cows were slow, sweetly foolish. One of the strange things about the chimooko-manag was that they took the cow's milk and drank it—this seemed, at first, disgusting to Omakayas. She hadn't believed such a thing when first she heard about it. However, the Break-Apart Girl seemed to enjoy the milk very much and even, once, sat down to nurse the cow with her hands and squirted the milk right into her own mouth! There was a pig, a gookoosh, who sighed and slept in the mud or snuffled at Omakayas. She was fascinated by his sensitive, wet, frantically rooting pink snout. There were two thick-furred sheep, and chickens. Omakayas very much wanted to have a chicken some day. Nokomis said that keeping these fat silly birds around to steal their eggs was one of the best chimookoman inventions that she knew of yet! For her part, the chimookoman girl was fascinated with Andeg, who had followed them and swooped down when he saw them eating. The girl fed the clever bird bits of apple and seemed to admire everything he did.

At last, Omakayas and Twilight turned to walk toward home. Before they left, the Break-Apart Girl held each of their hands. She spoke very quickly to them, insistently, in zhaganashimowin, the language of her people, and Omakayas and Twilight nodded politely and smiled back at her, as they always did, until she was satisfied. She seemed so lonely, so desperate for them to do *something*. What this *something* was, they hadn't figured out. No matter. She was always happy to see them, and they her, although Omakayas, looking down at the girl's feet, felt very sorry for them in those knifelike hard makazinan.

FOUR

THE RED DOG'S PUPPIES

The red dog was half wild and suspicious. She had hidden her puppies cleverly from all humans, except Old Tallow. Perhaps as a test to find whether they were worthy of the puppies, Old Tallow asked Omakayas and Twilight to find the red dog's den. Omakayas knew that Old Tallow would tame the puppies and raise them as she had raised her other dogs—to eat only from their own dish, to fight off all intruders, to help her hunt, to obey her utterly, to give their lives for her if they must.

Even now, Omakayas was sure that her cousin would be walking toward Old Tallow's. Sure enough, she soon met Twilight on the path to the fierce old woman's cabin.

They were each a little nervous as they neared the house—Old Tallow was always gruff and her moods were unpredictable. She had told them to be there when she fed her dogs so that they could follow the red one to her hiding place. Sure enough, as they entered the little clearing around her cabin, Old Tallow was sitting in her usual place, on her split log bench, smoking her stone pipe. She grunted her approval of the girls and carefully emptied her pipe, cleaned it, and replaced it in its own little leather bag. They breathed out easily, in relief. She was in a good mood, and even before Old Tallow parceled out the chunks of meat and guts that she fed her dogs, she gave each girl one of the hard lumps of maple sugar she was famous for sticking to the inside pockets of her ancient ragged dress.

"Howah! You have come! That is very good!"

The dangerous-looking wolf dogs sat calmly at attention exactly two steps away, where Old Tallow had taught them to sit. They watched every move she made. Six pairs of eyes followed each tiny gesture of her hands. Old Tallow divided the food for the dogs, with great precision and care, into each bowl. She fussily moved one lump here, another there, so that none of them would have more than another. The dogs narrowed their eyes as if they, too, were measuring. When she was satisfied, Old Tallow placed the bowls on the ground in a certain order known only to herself and her dogs. She stood back and

told the girls to do the same. There was a momentous pause.

"Wesineeg," she said to the dogs.

With a great simultaneous leap they were at the food, bolting it with huge gulps. The food was gone in two blinks. The dogs sat back, their pink tongues hanging out. They gave Old Tallow and the girls satisfied dog grins, and trotted away to their own business.

"Now, follow her!" Old Tallow pointed, and the two girls leaped after the red dog into the bushes.

At first, the red dog walked with a nonchalant gait, pretending that she didn't notice them at all. She stopped a few times, as though politely to let the girls pass, and when they didn't she grumpily dragged herself forward a few paces and sat down again. They waited. Now the red dog eyed them with impatience. She wanted to get to her pups! Why were these humans behaving in such an odd fashion! She became suspicious of the girls. Suddenly, with no warning, she dashed off.

Omakayas jumped after her, running, scrambling through brush, and squeezing between the tight growth of alder. But Twilight, perhaps on some instinct that only her sensitive nature could discern, stayed back. And she was right to do so, for after an awful chase through one bog and thickets of close-woven bushes, the red dog disappeared. Omakayas did her best to follow, but finally, sweating and bitten by flies, she decided to return to the clearing where she'd last seen Twilight. When she burst back through the brush, there stood Twilight, holding one of the puppies in her arms!

The red dog had decided to try to lead the girls away from her pups, to lose them in the dense brush, but Twilight's instinct had been to stay where she was and sure enough, as soon as their surroundings were quiet, the puppies appeared. Out of a hole hidden underneath some rocks, one and then another fat, hilarious puppy tumbled, almost directly at Twilight's feet.

Now the puppies looked at the girls comically, hoping that these big new animals were ready to play. There were three of them, and they were the best things the girls had ever seen—each of them was round-bellied, puppy-friendly, and as excited about the girls as they were about them. The red dog began to bark and growl wildly in alarm, and Old Tallow hurried toward them. Pleased, she scratched the red dog's head and told her that the girls were harmless. Suspicious, the red dog grumpily crouched at attention and watched every little move they made with motherly alarm.

"You have done good work," Old Tallow told the dog. "But now it is time for you to rest. Let others take care of your children. They *will* take *good* care of them." Old Tallow fixed the girls with a ferocious, squinting glare and they hurried to agree with her.

"Now," Old Tallow said to the girls, holding the red dog close to her, stroking her head, "you girls must choose. Use great care. This dog will depend on you for its life, and some day you may depend upon your dog for yours. So watch your puppy very closely. Look into its eyes to determine its character."

The girls pretended to give their choices a great deal of thought, but in truth they had already made up their minds. Twilight picked the one who had nearly jumped into her arms. He was a bold, affectionate gray. As for Omakayas, she stayed with the other two for a long time, but in truth, her puppy had already chosen her. Some black wolf with yellow eyes had been its grandfather, she was sure, and this puppy had the same quiet and alert nature as a wild animal. The little black male watched Omakayas for

54

a long while before finally he came over and sat next to her. Even after that, he really did not consent to play until sure that Omakayas was someone to be trusted.

Makataywazi, she named her dog, meaning the black one, black like her crow, Andeg. She held her dog, soft-furred, salty-smelling, puppy-sweet, very close as she carried him home. All the way there, her puppy was very quiet, but then as though he sensed that he was entering a new life he whimpered a little when they neared the house. As they came in sight, Andeg lifted off the top pole of the birchbark house and swooped down, curious. He wheeled high, his voice grating in alarm. *Crak! Crak!* What was his human carrying? The puppy strained from Omakayas's arms, taut with eagerness to play with the intriguing bird. When Omakayas let him down, he watched Andeg. The crow circled low, then pounced on the puppy's back and pecked the top of his head. Makataywazi yelped and then, as he was only a little puppy, he stumbled over his own feet and sprawled right on his face in front of Yellow Kettle, the very one who didn't like dogs! Omakayas had planned to introduce her new puppy slowly, displaying his charms to her mother carefully. But Andeg had decided otherwise. Yellow Kettle, who sat on the ground with Nokomis mending the fishing net, gave the puppy a resigned look and kept on working. Bizheens was sleeping right near them. Quietly Makataywazi sat between the two women and waited.

It was the right thing to do.

"Why, he's not such a bad little thing!" Mama noticed, and she even put out her hand to pet Makataywazi; at least she stroked him with one finger. That was all Mama said and all she needed to say. Obviously, she and Old Tallow had talked over the idea beforehand, because there was a little bowl of fish trimmings ready for the puppy. Omakayas scooped the dog up and brought him to the edge of the camp to feed, relieved to see that there was no Pinch anywhere in sight. She dreaded the sight of her brother, for he would immediately try to take over her puppy, she knew, and teach it to hunt and kill frogs for him. He didn't know the teachings of Old Tallow, who had trained her pack of dogs so well.

"Food is the only key, and you must use it wisely," Old Tallow had instructed her. "Never give food unless your dog does something to earn it, no matter how small. They need to have a job, just like us humans. That's why they have their own dishes, too. They are different, they are dog people, but they are after all a kind of people. And of all the many animals, they are the only ones who can stand to be around us."

THE BEAUTIFUL SLEEPWALKER

Angeline was so beautiful, even with the pits of small-pox that scarred her cheeks, that Omakayas some-times gazed upon her as on a striking sunset, or a particularly lovely bird in the woods, or an amazing piece of beadwork. It was very nice to look at her, and nobody's eyes ever got tired. Since her illness, Angeline had changed from a somewhat remote and haughty older sister to a person of deeper understanding. Although she was sometimes her old self, and hurt Omakayas's feelings, most of the time now she had patience with Omakayas. They talked like friends.

Since Fishtail had left, Omakayas could tell that something was wrong with Angeline. She wasn't ever hungry and merely picked at her dish of food until Pinch, eyeing whatever she had, begged her to let him finish it. She sighed as if a lump were in her chest. She swallowed hard as though the lump had moved to her throat. In her sleep,

she moaned. Sometimes Omakayas found her sister staring hard at the bark of a tree, not really seeing it, or she caught her sister in arrested motion with a needle in her hands, frowning into the air.

Omakayas knew that her sister's distraction had something to do with Fishtail's absence, but exactly what never occurred to her until Nokomis said, kindly, as the three worked together on a deer hide that would be sold to the trader, "Someone is thinking of someone far away."

Someone is thinking of someone. Angeline didn't even hear her grandmother, for she was staring just past the edge of the deer hide with a half smile on her face. Her arms worked, her hands scraped a sharp clamshell against the hide and removed the deer hair, but Angeline behaved as though she were a sleepwalker living in a dream. Nokomis smiled, and went on with her own work, but Omakayas put down her scraping tool and stared at her sister.

Someone is thinking of someone. One someone was Angeline, for sure. The other someone was not here, but far away. The only people far away were Deydey, who was just off hunting and who wouldn't make Angeline look so dreamy, and Pinch, but he was only at the other end of the island and he certainly wouldn't make her smile. And then there was Fishtail. For Angeline to look that way over Fishtail was certainly odd, but the answer of course was obvious once Omakayas put the two in one thought.

Angeline loved Fishtail. She sighed over him and missed him and wanted him to return. The recognition of her sister's feelings swelled Omakayas's heart. Her blood raced and she felt just a little faint. Love! It was a powerful thing, a grown-up and mysterious thing. The very idea of it made Omakayas instantly lonely. One day, she would lose her sister to Fishtail. Until then, this love that her sister felt didn't seem to make her happy. In fact, this love was a huge and serious weight on her shoulders. A worry. A nagging dream. Something that took her away from the present life.

Still, Nokomis smiled about it and indulged it, so it couldn't be a bad thing, could it?

Omakayas took up her scraper again and continued working on the hide. Her thoughts turned inward. Just that morning, she had dreamed that a voice told her, "Take the charcoal!" The voice was familiar, but the speaker was hidden. Take the charcoal. But how could that be?

Children who were ready to go off alone in the woods and fast for a vision took charcoal from the fire and blackened their faces with the crumbly ash. That way, people could see their intentions. When a boy or girl did this, a relative took that child into the woods and left him or her in a special place for four days and nights, sometimes more and sometimes less, with no food. The relative checked on the young person from time to time, for safety, but the child fasted in the hope that the spirits of the animals or of the winds, of the waters, the sky, the trees, would have pity on him or her.

A spirit who took pity on a child would choose to guard and protect that child all of its life. That spirit would speak in dreams. It would help the child when times were harsh. Looking for a guardian was an important thing, but frightening, too. Omakayas had already dreamed of her protector, the bear. Her bear spirit had come to her after the terrible winter when she lost her brother. She didn't need to fast. She was sure that she had suffered enough! Omakayas knew it was wrong, but she decided not to tell her mother or Nokomis about the dream. What if it meant that she must go back to the woods, alone?

"Ahneen, my sister!"

It was Pinch, returned from his supposed hunting trip with the other boys from the village. These days they often took off in packs to pretend they were mighty hunters. Once in a while they brought back a rabbit, more often only the exaggerated tale of a brave encounter. Along with their unreliable stories, they brought back a sack of berries or hard nuts, and so much energy that it spilled into the clearing with an abrupt explosion. But today, Pinch was strangely subdued. He walked casually toward his sister and even gave her a smile, nodding pleasantly.

"That looks nice," he said, pointing to her work. The unusual politeness of his remark should have warned

Omakayas immediately, but she didn't react quickly enough. With a swift movement Pinch reached into his shirt as he passed his sister, and with an even quicker jerk he grabbed the back of her dress and dropped something down it, something warm and cold all at once, something squirmy and panicky.

"Your namesake!" He crowed, darting from the clearing, glee in his shout. "Frog! Frog! Frog!"

Omakayas untied her belt and did a quick dance to free the huge frog, which landed, dazed, in an abject heap, then gathered its wits and leaped with one bound into Nokomis's lap.

Startled, Nokomis jumped up and knocked over a makuk of stew by her foot. The puppy, springing forward helpfully to lap it up, tangled himself in the fishing net, which had been hung to dry. Fighting to free himself, he rolled it into a tangle and then collapsed a rack hung with dried fish. When another dog, a strange dog attracted by the ruckus, hurled itself forward to grab the meat from the tumbling rack, the angry cries of Nokomis and Omakayas roused Yellow Kettle, who rushed from the birchbark house in confusion, dragging the belt she'd been weaving on a stick behind her. The stick caught in the doorway, slammed Yellow Kettle to the ground, and tore the birchbark.

Seeing what a mess his prank had caused, Pinch ran.

Omakayas didn't stop to help Nokomis pick the meat

up or put the frog in the woods, or certainly to face her mother's wrath. She leaped forward to chase her brother, and Makataywazi jumped after her with a puppy eagerness. Andeg, too, crowing with excitement, gave chase from tree to tree high above them. Omakayas darted down the path with vengeful joy. When she caught her brother she rolled him on the ground and threw handfuls of sticks and leaves into his face. Andeg flew down and attacked the puppy, poking, pecking, and flapping. The frightened puppy hid under a prickly bush and Andeg hopped furiously above in the leaves. Omakayas was unstoppable. She did not quit until she felt she'd got even. But by then she'd so thoroughly trounced her brother that his face was red, his lower lip trembled, he looked both proud and about to cry. She took pity on him.

"Ombay," she got up and beckoned to him to follow. She helped Makataywazi from his hiding place while Andeg croaked in protest. Even though Omakayas and Pinch were usually at war, there were moments of truce— now was one. They took off, kept on running into the woods until they were far enough away from home that they could say and do whatever they wanted.

"How come Old Tallow didn't give me a dog?" asked Pinch, looking enviously as Makataywazi. "Or Two Strike, either? She's mad about you getting a dog, you know."

"Neither you nor Two Strike found their den," said

Omakayas, but she knew that the truth was different. In the first place, Pinch, well, he was *Pinch*—bold, selfish, loud, thoughtless. He was a bad bet to take care of the children of Old Tallow's precious friends, and Two Strike the same. Besides that, Omakayas and Old Tallow had a special feeling between them. It was a cross between the feeling that Omakayas had for her mother and the way she felt about her grandmother. There was a little of the way she felt about her father mixed in too. Yet because Old Tallow was, unlike them, fearsome and unpredictable, the feeling was different. As a baby, Omakayas had been found and rescued by Old Tallow, and then adopted by Yellow Kettle and Mikwam. So besides the fact she owed her life to the tall hunter woman, Old Tallow was the first of the family she'd known. Around Old Tallow, she felt safe. Nothing could harm her, but of course, when Old Tallow was watching she had to do things right.

Do things right. There was always to much to do, and a proper way to do it. Would she ever live up to the perfections of her mother or Nokomis or her big sister, Angeline?

"I wish I was bigger," she mumbled to her brother.

"What?"

"You know. I wish I was better at everything—snaring, weaving, beading, dancing, making canoes, everything, like Angeline."

"Nah," said Pinch sturdily, "you're good like you are."

Then, because his words were too friendly for a fierce warrior such as himself, he frowned and looked angry. That didn't last long. He thought of something he wanted to talk about.

"You're always having dreams," said Pinch. "What's it like?"

Omakayas looked suspiciously at Pinch. How could he know that she'd dreamed this morning?

"What are you saying?" asked Omakayas.

"Dreams," said Pinch. "Dreams, sister. I don't want to have a spirit dream. I don't want to go out in the woods alone."

Omakayas now listened to her brother closely. Pinch looked at her with solemn consideration. Would she laugh?

"I don't think I'll ever do it," he whispered.

"Why not?" said Omakayas.

"I hate getting hungry," he said at last, in a very little voice. "It reminds me of that winter."

Besides living through the sickness during the terrible time two winters ago, food had been scarce. The whole family had got so hungry that they went to bed with their bellies stuck to their backs. They had walked around dizzy, and in their constant itching desire for food, they had chewed on bark and lichen. They even gnawed on pieces of old leather. Poor Pinch. He loved food more than anything ever after that. He grabbed food wherever he could and now his little belly was tight and round, and stuck out above the tie of his britches.

"Sometimes I think if I eat all I can, all summer, I'll store it up and I won't get hungry in the winter."

Omakayas couldn't help but smile, though Pinch was very serious. Pinch was such a mixture of brave and scared, of pretend warrior and his mama's baby. He irritated her to pieces and then, sometimes, he was the only friend whom she could trust.

"Me, I'm scared too," she said. "When I was given my dream about the bears, I was scared but, brother, it turned out well. I had more courage after that. Well, a little more, anyway."

Pinch was quiet. He sympathized with his sister now and took her very seriously. He was thinking.

"Sister," he said at last, gathering himself bravely, "do you think the spirits will get mad if you sneak some food to me out there?"

"I don't know," Omakayas said, gloomily, "but I know for sure Nokomis would be mad." She thought some more. "I can't do it," she said with regret. "Besides, it's not so bad going without the food. It's something else. . . ."

"What?"

Pinch only dreamed about ordinary things, about the kind of fish he might catch, about helping his father build a new jeemaan, about things he'd already done that day.

Mainly, he dreamed about food. He didn't have dreams that upset him or frightened him, except sometimes he dreamed he'd tripped, fallen off the jeemaan, out of a tree, down a cliff. He was always getting into accidents, even while he slept. In the morning, when Nokomis asked his dreams, he usually said something like "I dreamed there was another pot of stew" or "I was climbing that same tree and the branch broke again."

"I'm afraid of what I might dream," said Omakayas now, and from the look of incomprehension on Pinch's face she knew that her confession did not mean a thing to him. He couldn't be frightened of the bowls of corn or manoomin in his dreams, or the little bumps or scrapes he endured. Those were normal, and even better, when he woke he was always pleased to examine his arms and legs and find no bruises. There was no reason for Pinch to ever be afraid of his dreams.

FIVE

THE CANOE MAKERS

Now it was time to make jeemaanan. The whole family was working on the canoes that would carry them through the year. Birchbark jeemaanan were a big part of their livelihood. Sometimes the family sold them to the French voyageurs, or traders, who would pay a handsome price. But the jeemaanan they were making right now were for the family's use. Near Old Tallow's cabin two smooth cleared spaces held the makings—birchbark, cedar wood, jack-pine roots, pails and makakoon of water to use in soaking the roots. The cedar boat forms, like ribs, were weighted to the bottom of the jeemaanan with heavy stones. The long, wide strips of bark, taken from the oldest and smoothest birch trees, would soon take on pointed canoe shapes. Deydey and Old Tallow were hard at work today, gathering and softening enough jack-pine roots to sew the sides.

When he found the right jack-pine tree, Father offered a little tobacco, with thanks. Then he began to dig in the shade of the pine with Nokomis's iron hoe—the one she was proud of and guarded jealously. The roots followed the shape and direction of the tree branches, only they went under the ground. He lifted the roots up with his hands and a sharpened stick. When he had a nice long length, Father used his sharp hatchet to chop off the root. He took only a few roots from each tree so as not to hurt the tree. It was Pinch's job to gather the roots behind his father and to bring them to the bucket to soak.

Of course, that wasn't a manly enough job for Pinch.

While his father was down at the beach filling the pails, Pinch stealthily took the hatchet and with great whacks began to chop at a tree root. He used all his strength, but he couldn't sever the root. His efforts grew wilder, he chopped harder and harder, until at last in his frustration the hatchet slipped and Pinch gashed his own leg.

"Aaaaarooooooooh!"

Pinch's howl was earsplitting. Everyone heard it and came running. Omakayas gasped when she saw the blood running down his leg, but instinctively, as though she'd practiced, she did the right thing and made him lie down right where he was. Nokomis was there instantly. Gently, she rolled up Pinch's pants leg and directed Omakayas to fetch her medicine bag. As soon as Omakayas gave her the bag, Nokomis took out a small, tightly woven sack of powder and showed Omakayas how to press pinches of gray stuff to the side of Pinch's leg. He did not suffer in noble silence, but raved and kicked and howled on and on. Through it all, Omakayas stayed calm and pressed the powder on the wound until the bleeding stopped.

"There."

"Am I going to be a one-legged boy?" Pinch asked fearfully.

"Of course not." Omakayas and her grandmother exchanged a glance, trying not to smile. Pinch had such a wild imagination and always feared horrible outcomes to ordinary problems.

"You're going to stay a two-legged boy," his grandma assured him.

"Unless you steal your Deydey's hatchet again! If you do, I'll chop those legs off myself!"

It was Yellow Kettle. Fear often aroused her temper and to think what might have happened to her son terrified her into a rage. "You sit right there and don't you move!" That, usually, was the worst sort of punishment for Pinch. But his leg must have hurt, for he only smiled with a wan grace and lay himself back against a soft hummock of grass where he'd had the good luck to choose to collapse.

"I'll just watch," he said in a weak little voice.

Omakayas couldn't help but think that in spite of the pain, and now that he had squeezed the situation for all the sympathy possible, Pinch was enjoying the fact that he wouldn't have to help. Angeline was already hard at work again, softening and splitting the roots that she and Nokomis would use as the wondrously tough thread that would hold the jeemaanan together. Deydey was pounding stakes into the ground in the shape of the jeemaan. As he finished each stake, he bent the bark up into the form. This was crucial. Many a time he stood back with a narrowed eye and regarded the would-be jeemaan with a critical intensity. Old Tallow shared his solemn, thoughtful air. Every so often she filled her pipe and stared at the progress of the work. After long scrutiny, she made some tiny adjustment. They all worked equally on each of the two canoes. One was developing into the classic canoe shape, but the other, which would belong to Old Tallow, had a little roof in the stern of the boat.

"How come you're making your canoe like that?" asked Omakayas.

Old Tallow looked down at her, squinting one sharp eye. She said nothing. Omakayas knew her well enough to understand that when Old Tallow didn't want to answer a question, she did not evade or apologize. She didn't act as though she hadn't heard the question. And of course, she never lied. She just said nothing. Nothing. She let the silence between them fill the air. Unlike other people, Omakayas had noticed, silence did not make Old Tallow uncomfortable.

Now the warrior lady simply stood and smoked her pipe. The smoke drifted serenely in wavering fangs from each corner of her mouth. She was thinking. Omakayas did not ask the question again. Still, she wondered. Why the odd addition to her jeemaan? All around them, dogs sat panting in the shade, watching as the humans did yet another of the mysterious things they liked to do. Makataywazi was glad to get together with his puppy brothers and sisters, and they growled and mock-fought up and down the beach. All day, stopping only for a handful of rice or to douse themselves with icy water from the lake, the family worked. By the end of the day the stakes were in place. A huge amount of root was soaking, thanks to Yellow Kettle, who was even better than Mikwam at digging up the long, snaky jack-pine roots.

Omakayas and her grandma went down to the beach to haul in the net Yellow Kettle had set out that morning. They brought in a load of shining fish—jack fish, pike, a few trout with beautiful mottled skins and red gills.

Some of the fish they put on a basswood stringer and left in the water, away from the dogs, to clean and dry tomorrow. The other plump fish Nokomis immediately split open with the sharp knife she kept in a sheath at her belt.

Now it was getting dark. The fire danced up, shooting sparks into the night, reflecting in tiny moons of glitter on the waves. Nokomis tested one of the long green alder sticks, well peeled by a grumpy Pinch, who had thought he shouldn't have any chores at all. She poked the stick through half of the fish, then gave the fish to her granddaughter. Omakayas roasted her fish, the fat dripping in the fire and curling away from the meat in delicious black strings. Everyone did the same. They ate one fish after another, and then some more. Yellow Kettle even fed Bizheens tiny morsels. He cooed and smacked his little mouth. They picked every last bit of flesh from the bones, and then threw the spines and bones back into the water. That was to show respect for the fish so that they would allow people to keep catching them. Afterward, everyone lay back in the sand.

The air cooled quickly. It was a little cold to sleep outside, but Deydey spread out the fire and built it up to a huge blaze. When the fire had all burned down to a bed of coals, he spread out the coals and then all of the family heaped sand on top of the big spread-out remains of the fire. They were making their bed. The soft, comfortable sand was their mattress. Underneath, the coals would continue to give off a gentle heat. They all lay down under the stars. There were no mosquitoes or flies when the air was so chilly. Yet the warmth from underneath kept them comfortable. Deydey made this sort of sand bed often on his trips, and the children loved for him to make it for them.

As she lay back and looked into the shining blackness of the sky, Omakayas felt a huge sleepy comfort take hold of her. Makataywazi slept close enough for her to touch, fur soft and breathing quiet. Andeg roosted in the nearest tree and would wake her by gently tugging her hair in the morning. Their stomachs were full of roasted fish. Their minds were at peace. Underneath Omakayas, the sand radiated a soft warmth. She snuggled into it, her head pillowed. Those she loved were arranged around her, quietly talking or already asleep. The world felt whole and quiet, calm and safe. Omakayas drifted into her dreams.

SIX

THE RICING DISASTERS

It was time to go ricing again, and Omakayas was excited because this year she would knock rice—manoomin— while her mother used a long pole to push the jeemaan through the rice bed. All the years before, Mama had teamed up to rice with Angeline or Auntie Muskrat. But this year she told Omakayas that she was old enough and strong enough to help her, and Omakayas was very proud. The new jeemaanan were finished, the seams in the bark sealed with spruce gum, the last touches fussily applied by Deydey. Before they were launched for the first time, Nokomis burned sweet grass and fanned the smoke over them, praying softly. Omakayas knew that her grandma was praying that the jeemaanan would carry the family safely where they wished to go.

The canoes were loaded with sleeping blankets, rice knockers, new never-worn rice makazinan to use when dancing on the rice, and the beautiful mats and birchbark fanning baskets that Nokomis had made early that summer. Though so many of the men were traveling, the trip was still joyous. All the way to the ricing camps, Deydey, Yellow Kettle, and Nokomis sang traveling songs. Angeline struck the beautiful hand drum that Deydey had made for her. The beat helped them make good time by coordinating the strokes of their paddles, and they fairly flew across the water between the island and the rice camp. Andeg flew beside them, landing from time to time on the bow of the jeemaan for a rest on the crossing. Makataywazi had not been allowed to come and had stayed back with one of Mama's friends, who promised to feed him well. This made Andeg very happy. He had Omakayas all to himself, and he made the most of it by sitting on her shoulder, running his beak through her hair, and delicately accepting tidbits of food she took from the string bag at her waist.

Once they arrived at the rice camp, Omakayas tried to contain her excitement. There was so much to do. The place was a bustle of activity with everyone settling in and putting up their bark lean-tos, kindling cooking fires, gathering wood, rolling out blankets and sleeping mats.

The cousins were hauling water for their mothers, and as usual, Two Strike Girl was angry about the fact that she was asked to do women's work.

"I'm too strong for this!" She spoke with derision. Although in fact carrying the water was a heavy job, she wanted a more exciting task. "Sorry, girls, I'm going off to hunt," she growled. She adjusted the bow she always carried now, slung around her neck, already strung. She touched the arrows that she carried on her back in a deerskin quiver. She had made herself a special pair of britches and no longer wore a skirt. Omakayas and Twilight were stung by the arrogant ways of Two Strike and annoyed that she wanted to leave them with more work to do. They blocked her way.

"You think you're so important, Two Strike," Omakayas said, angry, "Mama asked me to knock rice this year, like a grown woman. What do you think of that?"

Two Strike just made a bored face. It was Twilight who reacted. She looked at Omakayas with both envy and annoyance. This was desertion! If Omakayas was knocking rice out on the water, she, Twilight, would surely be left behind. She would have to babysit, to take care of the little ones. Still, she stuck by Omakayas as Two Strike struck a warrior's pose and spoke. "What of it? I'm going to get meat. What do I care what you little ladies do?" Two Strike stalked off with great determination, and for a while they could hear her tramping through the brush.

"She won't get anything that way," said Twilight, "she's too loud."

Omakayas laughed as they hauled the water toward camp, but the dismay on the face of her dearest cousin had upset her. She felt selfish leaving Twilight back with the babies, and in her guilt she got an idea.

"Let's go out ourselves, before the grown-ups, and surprise them."

"What?" Twilight was so shocked she put down her water pail. "We can't do that. Nobody can start until the rice boss says to start. We'd get in trouble!"

"If we were just coming back with a jeemaan full of manoomin, do you think they'd really scold us? They'd praise us because we proved how hard we can work!"

Omakayas was carried away with the romance of her idea. In her mind's eye she saw only triumph, a return in which she was the center of attention.

"We'll get in trouble," Twilight repeated stubbornly.

Their arguing went back and forth through the day, and on into the evening, until finally Twilight gave up. She told Omakayas that if she really had to do this thing she'd help, even though she didn't agree.

"I suppose," she said unwillingly, but loyal, "if you've made up your mind to get in trouble, I should get in trouble along with you."

By then, Omakayas was beginning to doubt that her idea was really all that good. When Twilight finally gave in, her victory didn't make her as happy as it would have made her at the beginning of the day. Still, she accepted her cousin's generosity and they agreed to meet at the shore, by Old Tallow's jeemaan, just before Sagachiwe, the red and glowing spirit who comes up every day to make sure the world is safe for the sun, appeared at the end of the lake.

Only the very earliest of morning birds were calling when the two girls woke. Stepping carefully, they sneaked away from the banked fire and made their way down to the shore. Omakayas held a pair of bawa'iganakoog, or rice knockers, very nice ones that her father had made. Twilight carried a long pole made from a straight, thick sapling that had split at the top into legs; it would help the girls to push along the mud bottom of the shallow lake. Without a word, the two launched Old Tallow's jeemaan. She favored the two of them and wouldn't get angry if things went wrong. Not that Omakayas let herself think of failure! They shivered in the chill air, and the laden rice stalks brushed stiffly against them as they made their way from camp. When they were far enough out, just where the rice was thickest, before the sun had even risen, Omakayas began. With one wooden rice knocker, she bent a few stalks over the boat. With the other, she stroked and lightly struck the plants, dislodging the rice grains that clattered softly onto the bark bottom.

Very soon, the bottom of the boat was covered with rice and Twilight, poling carefully, brought them quietly to another area of the lake, where they continued their work. The sun's rays now sprayed a fierce radiance over the horizon, and touched them with the first light. Omakayas had just bent a fresh bunch of stalks over the jeemaan and began to knock when the boat rocked wildly. The rice plants surged, a great dark form rose beside them dripping weed and water.

Too shocked to even gasp, the two girls froze in place. A huge bull moose, with grand, heavy, curved antlers, stood in silhouette against the dawn sky.

Passing them without notice, as though they were bugs on the water, it heaved itself along and then suddenly, *thwock*. The girls heard the sound of the arrow released, and the sound of its striking force as one. The moose reared forward onto a sand bar in one immensely powerful lunge, then collapsed.

Howah!

It was Two Strike's unmistakable, shrill, triumphant shout.

Quickly, the girls poled to shore and beached the jeemaan. Their work went unnoticed, for the entire camp now was roused by Two Strike's thrilled dancing energy. She couldn't contain herself. She waded out to check her moose while the men of the camp were still rubbing the sleep off their faces.

"One arrow!" Two Strike crowed so all could hear. "One shot."

And it was true, her arrow had entered the eye of the moose at the exact right angle to strike deep into its brain.

"Could anybody but Two Strike be so lucky?" Omakayas muttered to Twilight under her breath. At the same time, she was ashamed not to make more of her cousin's unbelievable feat. It was just that she'd been so determined to gain respect for her work, much humbler though it was, more predictable. And now that Two Strike had killed the moose, there would be talk of nothing else.

Or so she soon wished.

For after the moose was dragged to shore and with great amazement and laughter Two Strike's family began to skin it right there, Mama and Auntie Muskrat discovered what their daughters had done. They weren't happy. As a matter of fact, it was worse. They were furious.

"You will not be helping me at all this year," said Mama, her face tight. She was controlling her temper, Omakayas could see, and she was glad there were so many others around right then. Deydey came to her.

"Namadabin." Omakayas sat at his command. Her father sat across from her and a stillness grew between them, not a pleasant stillness. She knew that he was thinking, choosing his words carefully, and they would not be words of praise.

"You struck the manoomin too green into your boat," he said abruptly, "ruining the plants. My daughter, there is a way we do things. We do it to take care of the rice. We listen to the old people—they who check the rice and watch for the exact right moment for us to humbly accept the gift. You went against the way things are supposed to go. You didn't listen to your old ones, your own grandmother among them."

Deydey frowned, and Omakayas's face burned. Her heart was stuffed with prickles of shame. Tears pushed against the backs of her eyes and she held her breath against them. She wouldn't cry and she wouldn't say she was wrong. The rice had fallen easily from the stalks, the lake was generous. She believed that her grandmother wouldn't be so harsh with her, nor would Old Tallow.

And it was true. Nokomis did not scold her. Old

Tallow didn't say a word or ever acknowledge that the two girls had taken her jeemaan and filled the bottom with rice. She emptied the boat. As the girls saw her doing it they pitched in and helped without a word. Nobody else spoke harshly to them, either. Perhaps it was obvious to all in the camp that their cousin's triumph was punishment enough. Two more days passed before the elders said that the rice was ready to be picked, and in those two days Two Strike Girl was given such a feast that it would be talked of for years. This sort of thing just didn't happen—a girl making a grown male warrior's shot. And there were those who predicted unusual things for Two Strike. Those who insisted that she was blessed in some way.

Omakayas was ashamed that she resented Two Strike. All she heard was Two Strike did this and Two Strike did that. Pinch followed Two Strike around like a puppy. Even Twilight seemed impressed by Two Strike's feat. When she overheard Nokomis say something admiring about Two Strike, a hollow place formed in Omakayas's heart. It wouldn't have been so bad if Two Strike had shared her glory, or at least been kind. But she was more arrogant than ever and now, for sure, nobody expected her to do women's work. Not anymore. Two Strike was free. Free to hunt while Omakayas turned rice over a hot fire. Free to fish while Omakayas hauled water and stacked wood beside the cooking fire. Free to do whatever she liked while Omakayas looked after the littlest children and made sure they did not burn themselves or wander off. As the days passed, Omakayas looked forward for the first time to leaving the rice camp, and heading back to the island.

The wind changed, and Old Tallow said new weather was sure to follow. Sure enough, the next morning there was a storm on the horizon. Everyone decided to leave quickly. The camp broke up in haste. Reed bags, makakoon, all sorts of containers filled with rice were shoved into piles. The babies were quickly bundled into the jeemaanan, the blankets rolled and stuffed around the youngest.

Deydey and Angeline left first, carrying the newly harvested rice. Everyone was worried that the rice would get wet, for mold would spoil it. Deydey and Angeline went ahead to race the wind and rain to pack the rice away. Soon everything in Old Tallow's and Mama's jeemaanan was ready. Nokomis and Omakayas had wedged in the last bundle. They were ready to go, but Pinch was nowhere to be found. He answered no call, and Mama's yells were very loud. Everyone assumed that he had jumped in along with Deydey and Angeline. By now, he was already back at the island.

The jeemaanan shoved off while the sky was still clear. As soon as they were on the water, they could see the ominous tinge of yellow-green just northwest that meant the storm was blowing off the land. It was tough to paddle across. The wind rose and the waves broke rough, white-capped, angry-looking. Several times, Omakayas was jolted with a thrill of fear when the jeemaan, pounded by an especially big wave, twisted and bucked high, then smacked down. They plowed on.

As they neared shore, Yellow Kettle put tobacco in the water in thanks for a safe crossing. All of a sudden there was a great pause as though the earth itself took a breath. A low stirring of thunder sounded. Nokomis, too, took from the pouch at her waist a pinch of tobacco and began to pray. Omakayas saw Deydey's jeemaan on shore, but no Pinch.

"He's probably helping pack away the rice at the house," said Mama. What a look of despairing shock crossed her face when they arrived at the island, pulled their jeemaan to shore, and Angeline came hurrying down to help.

"Where's Pinch?" she said.

"We all thought he was with you!" cried Mama.

"Oh yai!" Nokomis clapped her hands to her face and Omakayas immediately began to throw their cargo from the boat. Mama gave Bizheens to Nokomis and pulled the jeemaan back into the water. "He's left behind! I'm going back there!"

Deydey was at the cabin, caching the wild rice, and to fetch him back to travel across now would waste precious time. Usually, nobody argued with Yellow Kettle once she made up her mind, but Omakayas and Angeline tried. It was useless.

"Get away from me," she said.

Old Tallow growled louder than the thunder. "You can't go!"

With that, the ferocious old woman actually tried to yank the paddle from Yellow Kettle's hands. She had no luck. Yellow Kettle's eyes caught fire and she wrenched the paddle away.

"Daughter," Nokomis ordered, her voice stern. "Our friend Old Tallow is the only one who can make it across now. You have your baby to think about. Give her that abwi—now!"

Omakayas and Angeline gaped. Never before had they heard Nokomis order their strong-minded mother around, and never before had the voice of their kind grandmother sounded so forbidding. Her words got through to Yellow Kettle. With a worried look, she handed the carved cedar paddle to Old Tallow. Overhead, the sky had gone entirely blue-black and the binesiwag, or thunderbirds, were flashing their eyes and clapping their wings just over the trees of the mainland. Going back onto the water was dangerous.

"If anyone can make it, Old Tallow can," said Nokomis. "Let her be."

"I'm going too!" Omakayas yelled this with all the purpose she could muster. She thought of how Pinch's face had looked when he told her how frightened he was of being alone in the woods. What would he do when he returned to the camp and found no one there? Her heart squeezed painfully in sympathy for him. Even though he drove her crazy, she could not let him stay in the dark woods. Old Tallow got into the jeemaan, and Omakayas pulled herself in as well. As she did so, she caught a glance from Old Tallow that signified admiration, she was sure of it. She was so hungry for approval from Old Tallow that her heart swelled and she hardly noticed the paddle coming. But as Old Tallow expertly turned the boat and started off, she managed to cup the abwi under Omakayas. With one powerful movement, she neatly flipped Omakayas right out of the boat into the water!

More shame! Wading to shore, miserable, Omakayas helped carry rice bundles and would not meet anybody's eyes. Nokomis kindly said to her, "Omakayas, you are a good sister, but we wouldn't have let you go."

The clouds rolled closer and darkened. Omakayas turned and saw that already Old Tallow had moved past the farthest spit of island land, paddling as expertly as the strongest warrior. All of a sudden a rough gust of wind plucked the old woman's hat off and sent it whirling. Omakayas saw it bounce across the waves and hit shore. She ran after it, picked it up, and was afraid. The little flicker, or moningwanay feather that represented the strength of Old Tallow, had blown out of the hatband and into the rough, cold lake. The sharp black and yellow feather held as much power in it as an eagle feather. Omakayas watched Old Tallow disappear. She watched the storm approach. Holding Old Tallow's hat, she asked the binesiwag for pity.

"Don't strike her with the flashes from your eyes, don't pitch her over with your breath. Protect her and protect my little brother," she begged as she sprinkled tobacco on the shore.

Then, in spite of the threatening sky and thunder, she went looking for the little feather. The waves swooped in furiously, raised an angry green foam. Still, Omakayas searched. It seemed to her a sign from the binesiwag when, riding the tip of a wave, she saw the small black arrow of the feather. She plucked it from the water before it swirled back. Almost immediately, the brilliant yellow bands on its sides dried clear. Beneath the black clouds a shaft of sun pierced the sand with a sudden and fierce radiance. Then the cloud moved and the light went out. The storm was upon them.

The violent weather continued all day, and Old Tallow did not return. In their birchbark house, Omakayas tended the central fire. Many storms passed over. The southern thunderbirds were very powerful and Omakayas imagined them, flashing eyes and great crashing wings, as they approached through the darkening sky. Usually, she loved storms and never feared them. But today she was terrified for Pinch and Old Tallow. Nokomis covered the shiny pails and the little mirror, so as not to accidentally attract a binesi. The thunderbirds liked shiny things, but if those things were covered and tobacco was offered, they would pass over without hurting the Anishinabeg. Omakayas had to go outside at last, so she and Nokomis cut a few hemlock boughs, laced them tightly, and sat down against the trunk of a large birch tree. It was well-known that the birch tree was never struck by lightning because it was blessed by the great teacher of the Ojibwe, Nanabozho.

Omakayas also took care of Bizheens. As though he knew there was something wrong, he often reached out to touch Omakayas's face with his tiny hands. He patted her as though he were trying to comfort her, and he smiled at her hopefully.

"Little brother," crooned Omakayas, stroking and holding the tiny one, "wildcat boy, lynx baby."

He tipped his head toward her and snuggled just under her chin. The two fell asleep that way, and in the night, when Omakayas woke, with the wind blowing and Pinch still not home, she was very glad for his presence. She was glad that her mother let them cuddle close. Omakayas's eyes grew heavy, but before she dropped back into sleep she saw that Yellow Kettle had stayed up, next to the fire, watching over her little family and praying for her child's safe return.

All the next day, the wind blew steadily and mightily until it turned the lake into a froth of whitecaps. The dull, hollow unending roar sawed at Omakayas's nerves. Finally, without asking anyone's permission, she threw her blanket around her shoulders and slipped out, walked the path into town, and then waited onshore for the return of her brother. But the wind did not let up. Andeg could not battle it and he huddled in her arms, pecked at and worried the edges of her blanket. All Omakayas got was a deep chill. When the sky went dark, she had to admit that even Old Tallow would not cross the water. Sorrowing, she made her way home.

That night, sitting close to Nokomis, she could only stare miserably into the flames and wish for sleep to blot away her thoughts. The hat she was used to seeing on Old Tallow's head hung beside the door, the feather jutting out stiffly. Omakayas took comfort in that and, whenever her thoughts became too agitated, she looked at the feather. The wind moved in the trees, gnashing and growling in the pines like an animal. It seemed, in fact, even stronger than the night before. When at last she did fall asleep, she dreamed. Her dream was of her brother.

There was Pinch. To her surprise, he was working very hard, moving rocks. He was trying to get into a rabbit's hole. For some reason, he was very tiny, but also very strong! "Watch me!" he yelled in the dream. Omakayas saw that lazy Pinch could carry the great pale red boulders that were blocking his way. He hoisted them one after the other on his shoulders, and walked to the edge of the water. He tossed the stones in, and then turned around and stood. He looked at Omakayas. He was waiting for his sister to admire him. But in the dream, Omakayas just teased.

"You are just a little nuisance anyway, no matter how many huge rocks you carry!" As she said this, Omakayas woke, and when she remembered the whole dream she buried her face in her blankets, ashamed of herself. How could she be so mean! Her poor brother was missing! All he wanted was a kind word from her, and in the dream she'd laughed at him. It took a long time for her to fall back asleep, but when she did, she slept very deeply. The sun was risen and the day begun before she rubbed her eyes and crawled from her blankets. The first voice she heard, outside the lodge, was that of Old Tallow.

"Meegwech!" Next she saw the big, tough hands of the old woman reach into the skins across the door. The face poked in for a moment, and then the hat was gone. Omakayas bolted from her blankets and ran out of the lodge, too late to see Old Tallow lope away. There was Pinch sitting next to Deydey, a makuk of stew in his hands. Before she even thought about it she had put her arms around him. Her heart bounced up, she was so happy to see him.

"Quit that!" Pinch twisted away and spoke gruffly, but it was clear that he was hiding a smile. He was glad to see her too.

"What happened?" She sat with him, so glad to see him that she ignored the annoying slurping noises he made, on purpose as always, eating his stew.

"I guess Old Tallow got lost!" he said. "It's a good thing I found her! She was out in the woods. I was hauling rocks, when she suddenly wandered near to me."

Omakayas put her hand over her mouth and let him finish his stew in peace. Looking up, she saw that Mama and Nokomis were silently laughing with her. Of course, Old Tallow had found Pinch in the woods and then brought him home. Probably, as was usual with the fierce lady, she had hardly spoken two words to the little boy. Pinch had no idea that he'd even been left behind. He thought that *he* had saved Old Tallow! Angeline heard too, and she motioned Omakayas off. The two sisters went down the path to laugh about how Pinch interpreted his rescue. Only later in the morning, when she had a chance to think about her dream, did Omakayas realize that Pinch had said he was doing exactly that—hauling rocks. She'd dreamed accurately, but she said nothing about it.

MORE MOOSE DISGRACE

As if it weren't bad enough that Two Strike bragged about her moose kill and paraded around and considered herself a great hunter, Omakayas was given the job of tanning the hide of that very moose! Two Strike's family had divided up the meat long ago—it was eaten at the rice camps and what was left was dried in strips and carried back in that moose hide. Then the hide was softened in water. Nokomis dragged it out of the water and the rotten smell of it made Omakayas pinch her nose shut. It stank like crazy.

"Sorry, you'll have to use those hands," Nokomis laughed. "Weeji'ishin! Help me out! This thing is heavy."

With a dark look at the moose, which she resented for letting her cousin kill it, Omakayas grabbed a slimy, gamy corner and tugged it over to the log where they would work. Her father had given her a very good hide scraper made out of one of his own old gun barrels. It was one of those gifts Omakayas had tried hard to appreciate.

"I hate this mangy old moose hide," Omakayas blurted out. "Why doesn't Two Strike tan it herself?"

"The family gave us the hide of that first kill," said Nokomis, "because they know I'll make them something special."

Omakayas helped her grandmother drape the hide over the log that Deydey had set up. First they took turns using a scraper to remove all the hair. Then came the long hours of working the skin back and forth on the log to soften it. Nokomis was tireless. As she worked, she sang. Only her songs kept

Omakayas from running away from this task. As soon as she knew that Omakayas was doing the work, Two Strike would find a chance to tease her and sneer, as she always did: "Good little woman. Do your woman's work. Me, I'll go and hunt."

"Keep singing, Nokomis, please?"

Maybe her grandmother's songs would keep the irritations of Two Strike from her thoughts. The song said: Do not worry, my daughter, I am hurrying to make your makazinan before the snow falls!

DAGWAGING

FALL

SEVEN

THE RABBIT BLANKET

The sun lost its strength, leaves fell from the trees. There was still no word from Fishtail or the others who had left, and although life went on in its usual routine, there was an increasing tension under everything that people did. As she folded up the blankets, as she rolled up the birchbark strips and scoured the summer's pots and makakoon clean with sand, Omakayas couldn't help but wonder whether this would be the last time they would move from their summer camp to their winter cabin on her beloved island. And what about the woods, her special hiding places, the play camp beneath the willow, and the tree that Andeg made his special territory? Was she doing these special chores for the last time? By next summer would everything change?

Omakayas took reassurance where she could. Some things stayed the same. Town meant school for Angeline, work for Deydey, reliable company for Mama and Nokomis, and the security of log walls. Omakayas loved the cedar cabin that her family moved to every fall, right near the town of LaPointe. A pine tree gently murmured right outside the door. A set of stands for the jeemaanan were set up beside the kind tree. There were neighbors, the trading post, excitement, gatherings and dance. Anytime they wanted, they could trade in LaPointe and visit the interesting buildings of the chimookomanag. It took a lot of work to get the cabin ready, but the work was pleasant. As Omakayas and Angeline pressed mud into the cracks between the logs, Omakayas tried to still her thoughts. She wouldn't think past this winter, as winter was always hard enough. They would be glad they'd done a good job stuffing the cracks when the winter's icy winds blasted off the huge lake around them. They put down new floor mats and the tanned skins from all of their summer work. They made the inside of the cabin neat and snug.

Out in back, Deydey dug a huge hole and Nokomis lined it with birchbark. This would be the food cache. Dried corn, wild rice, beans, squash, and makakoon of maple sugar were carefully wrapped in bark. Mama and Nokomis tied those bundles tight. Then Deydey put that food deep inside the hole, and stuffed each package tightly around with beach grass. Omakayas dug potatoes and put them in last of all. Nokomis blessed the cache and Mama and Deydey sealed it up. In the depth of winter, they would draw from that store.

After the cache was buried, Nokomis sat down in the shade of the pine to finish weaving a rabbit-skin blanket for Omakayas. This blanket would be ready by the time the weather got really cold. For a year, the two had been snaring waaboozoog and preparing the rabbit skins. Now they had a huge pile. Omakayas had twisted each skin into a long furry rope. When she had enough rabbit-skin ropes, Nokomis wove them in and out and make the blanket. Now that it was nearly done, Omakayas watched her grandma tie off the edges. She could not wait to wrap herself within the fluffy blanket. No other child she knew had a rabbit-skin blanket. She knew that her grandmother was making this gift because there was a special love between them.

The love between Nokomis and Omakayas had to do with the things that Nokomis was teaching her every day about her plants and roots and medicines.

"Ombay," said Nokomis to her now. Omakayas stood up and Nokomis held out the blanket. Omakayas walked into it and put her face against the silky fur. "There will be plenty of time to enjoy this gift," said Nokomis. "For now, roll it up and put it in your sleeping corner. I need your help in the woods. Let's go."

Omakayas looked up into her grandmother's face. Her skin was creased like the finest doeskin, and her smile created a fan of pleasant wrinkles. Nokomis's deep eyes searched out and saw everything. Such clear sight did not frighten Omakayas, for what her grandmother saw she always forgave. Nokomis had never said a mean word to her in all of her life, had never even raised her voice. If she ever got exasperated or angry, the most that Omakayas saw her do was to utter a short hiyn! and turn away. Nokomis lived by the teachings of the Midewiwin. The most important human quality was kindness. After Omakayas put her special blanket away, the two walked into the woods.

Nokomis was looking for puffballs. The small round mushrooms dried out over the summer and contained a special powder that was ready in the fall. The brown silky powder was blessed by the ginebigoog, the snakes, and it was good medicine. It had many uses, including the healing of cuts and scrapes. This was the powder that Nokomis had pressed on Pinch's leg when he'd chopped himself with Deydey's hatchet. The powder was sprinkled on the umbilical cords of new babies, and it cleared up any rashes and sores Bizheens suffered. The puffballs were also great fun, though Omakayas did not mention that. She and her cousins loved to find these old dried puffballs in the spring and have fights with them. When squeezed, the puffballs popped open and squirted out the powder with a little blast. They had little puffball wars. It was a waste of good medicine, but because she was one of these puffball-squeezing children Omakayas knew just where lots of the little round mushrooms grew.

She took her grandmother there, and when she pointed out the area Nokomis clapped her hands together in delight, for she was enormously pleased to see so many all at once.

"Meegwech, meegwech," she said excitedly, then put a pinch of tobacco on the earth, prayed, and thanked the

spirits for providing these medicines. Omakayas began to pluck the tiny wrinkled round skins from the ground. She worked carefully, sealing up the hole on top with her finger to keep in the powder, while she gently pulled it from the ground. The work was pleasant. Above her, the pine needles sighed together and gossiped softly in the wind. All around, the insects trilled their good-byes to the summer sun. The birds occasionally uttered their travel calls or warning songs to one another. Makataywazi, with her as always, sat in the shade of a bush. Above them,

Andeg occasionally appeared to watch them, but he was wilder these days, different. He was preparing to travel away from the island, south, and spend time with more of his own kind.

As Omakayas worked with her grandmother, a pleasant silence grew around them. At last, it was time to quit. They sat on a comfortable old, round log. "Weesinidah," said Nokomis. She took some dried meat and berries from the bag at her waist. As she shared it with Omakayas, she told her about something that had happened to her as a child.

THE LITTLE PERSON

Watch closely, my granddaughter, for this is the time of year when they appear, the memegwesiwag, the little people. They are preparing for winter, just like we do. They gather medicines and store up their food. I was a little younger than you when I saw one of them, and I have never forgotten him, for he saved my life then, and ever since, he has helped me in many ways!

Omakayas settled closer. In the sweetness of the sun there was already a winter chill. Although she knew the story, she loved to hear about her grandmother's helper.

I was raised by my grandparents, said Nokomis, we stayed far off in the woods, away from other people. Alone out there, you see things. I learned so much out there. Nimishomis, my grandpapa, he treated me like his son and took me everywhere with him. He taught me what he'd normally teach a boy—how to fix arrows and hunt down moose, how to capture an enemy with a rawhide snare, how to sneak up on a deer, even how to play a love flute! He taught me how to read tracks in the snow, and signs on trails. I could always tell which animals had passed, and exactly what they were thinking and doing.

Still, although he taught me so much, there came a time when I got lost in the woods.

At first, I would not admit that I had gone too far in checking my snares. But I had followed some delicious-looking berry bushes. I got turned around, couldn't backtrack, couldn't find my way. So I kept on, trudging through the brush, making my way deeper and deeper into unfamiliar territory, until at last I had to admit that I was lost. When I realized this, I sat down where I was and I must confess that I began to cry. Sadness overcame me. I believed that I would die, all alone, and I felt very sorry for myself and for my grandparents. What would they do?

Fortunately, it was summer. I knew a little bit

about how to survive. I made myself a shelter out of basalm branches. I owned a small fire-steel and I struck a fire from it. Maybe I could snare a duck or two, or trap fish, I thought. Perhaps, before winter came, my grandparents would track me down. There was hope, and I decided to take hold of that hope.

After I decided not to fall into despair, I began to look around. I explored my surroundings, and that was when I happened upon something very interesting. I always examined the mud near the stream to see what animals had come to drink. Often, I saw the trails of otters. I loved to spy on them and watch them tickle their young and flip over and slide down the riverbanks. I loved to see the comical, curious, laughing expressions on their faces. That morning, I saw no tracks of otters, but I did see something unusual.

There in the mud a tiny human footprint, the small track of a child, was pressed. I measured it—not even as big as my palm! I became very curious, for the foot was as small as a baby's, a fat baby's. It was a broad little footprint. But if it was a baby, surely it couldn't walk yet, and this being was very nimble. I followed the steps and found that not only did the child walk, but skipped, hopped lightly, and ran with great delicacy across uneven ground. Rain had just stopped, so here and there I could find a series of tracks. I was intrigued by their baby size and amazed by the strength and grace they showed. I was, in fact, so absorbed in tracking this being that I was amazed when right before my nose, as I knelt, I saw a tiny makazin and heard a piping and amused laugh.

"Mighty tracker!"

To my amazement, I looked up into the face of a little person just as perfect as any man, only hairy like a chimookoman. His clothing was of fine tanned deerskin, quilled in the old way, not beaded.

"Mighty tracker!" He addressed me again, very amused at my intent examination of his footprints. "You have found me. Now, what are you going to do?"

He had a sweet little crinkled face, round as a berry and very dark, with bow lips and shining eyes. He was tinier than my little brother, who was only three years old at the time. Yet there was something huge about him. He awed me, and my heart began to pound so hard I could not speak.

"Don't be afraid," he said, his voice kind,

"I am always around. You just haven't tracked me before."

I was still very much afraid, but I had a tiny pinch of tobacco in the pouch at my waist, and this I laid at his feet, wishing I had something else to give him. However, he was mightily pleased with this.

"Meegwech, meegwech, you are a very good girl, I thank you! In return for this tobacco, I'm always going to help you. Don't worry about a thing, my girl, I'll look after you when times are difficult."

I blinked and he was gone, but the sighting of this little person filled me with a good feeling, and it wasn't long after that my grandparents found me. After that, I had more confidence.

My grandparents noticed the difference, and when I told them about the little person I had spoken with they were very happy about it. "Those little people love the Anishinabeg, and we love them. So this visit you had was a very good thing!"

We were to find out just how good it was in the

coming winter, when times got tough indeed.

How sad it was that winter. The snow fell very deep, there was no game to be found, and a family that we knew was drifted over with snow and starved to death in their wigwam. They were found stone cold around the ashes of their fire when the snow melted, all of them curled up as if going to sleep. My grandparents were desperate to survive, for they knew my brother and I were incapable of taking care of ourselves just yet. Every day, in spite of the fact that he was old and weak, Nimishomis got out his bow, which he was hardly strong enough to shoot, and he went hunting. Nokomis and I gathered wood and checked our snares for rabbits. More often than not, however, the loops hung empty.

We were thinking of stewing up our own makazinan one day, and eating the tough leather, when I went out alone, without my grandmother, to check a snare where I had had luck before. Sure enough, as I approached I saw a rabbit. However, he was sitting by the snare just waiting for me, too smart to go inside.

"My child," he spoke to me as I looked at him, weak with hunger, "do not set your snares so carelessly. Also, watch my tracks." He bounded off and I resolved that in spite of my dizzy head I'd take more care with my nooses from then on. I looked down, expecting to follow rabbit tracks, but instead and to my surprise I saw that the tracks that the rabbit left were the tracks of a tiny person.

Of course, I followed them.

I followed those tracks deep into the bush, unafraid of getting lost. With the snow on the ground, I could always backtrack. Besides, even weak as I was I wanted to see my friend again, to speak with my memegwesi, my little helping spirit. But he eluded me, stayed ahead of me, never quite let me see him, and after a while of tough going I began to understand that he was leading me toward something.

Many times, I fell to the ground in my weakness, to rest. I ate a handful of lichen once, gathered more for a soup that my grandparents could share, stuffed my blanket full. I was nearly at the end of my strength when, with great excitement in his voice, my memegwesi called me from the top of a mound. I looked, saw the little man waving at something on the ground, and by the time I had clambered up to where he crouched, he had disappeared. There, however, right where he had pointed, was a thin swirl of steam. A little melted spot where breath escaped. The sign of a sleeping bear.

That bear was easily killed in its deep sleep, my girl. The meat and fat saved us that winter, and the skin of that bear kept me warm in our lodge. I still carry one claw of that medicine bear in my pouch. I have seen my little memegwesi helper once since—another story. Mi'iw minik. That is all.

Only much later, returning with Grandmother and the makuk full of puffballs that would help in her healing work, did Omakayas remember that Nokomis told stories for a reason. This one she had told, about her helping spirit, was a clear message. The message was, of course, that it was time for Omakayas to go and seek instruction and protection from her own spirits. But not yet, thought Omakayas, not yet. Please? Soon. Not now!

ANGELINE'S ZHOONIYAA

Omakayas, worn out, sat onshore watching her sister toil with the net. Even though it was late afternoon and the sun was low, the air chilled, and they had been fishing all day, Angeline was setting the net out once more in the hope of another catch. If this kept on, they would be cleaning fish by the light of a bonfire!

"You're crazy," Omakayas grumped, knowing her adored older sister was too far out in the water to hear her.

"And I'm all tired out and cold. I'm leaving."

Just as Omakayas rolled over and tried to sneak around the rocks into the trees and undergrowth, down the path home, Angeline swooshed to shore and with a loud call apprehended her little sister. But the taste of freedom was too much for Omakayas. She barely paused at her sister's shout.

"Get back here!"

The order from her sister only hardened Omakayas. All day, she'd been helping her sister with the fishing. Angeline was doing something extra, to get money for some private purpose, other than her family's needs. Without asking a single question, Omakayas had helped. Now all she got in return was an angry shout. She plunged for the branches of the first trees.

"Please, oh please," Angeline hurried after. "You know I can't do it alone."

"Well you *sound* like you can do it alone!" Omakayas turned slightly, frowned at her sister, and went on.

"I can't, really, oh please. I mean thank you. Meegwech."

"What did you say?"

"I said thank you. Meegwech, sister." Humbled, Angeline stood beside Omakayas now. "You've been working right beside me all day, You've helped me, sister." There was an awkward pause as Omakayas waited for Angeline to tell her the reason for her mysterious flow of energy.

"What do you need the zhooniyaa for?" she finally asked.

"Something . . ." Angeline's voice trailed off vaguely.

Omakayas turned away again. She was hungry. She was annoyed. Angeline did not follow. Did she think that she was keeping a secret about her love for Fishtail? No doubt, she wanted the money from the extra fish in order to buy something nice for him. Maybe she wanted to make him a jacket like the chimookomanag wore, or some new makazinan. Maybe she wanted to buy beads. It was obvious that it had to do with Fishtail. Why couldn't Angeline just come right out and say so?

"I'm not a baby, you know," yelled Omakayas.

"I know you're not. You really helped me. Look. Two bales dried." She waved her hand back at the packs of fish they had caught together, skinned and filleted together, smoked and dried together, and now argued over together. Omakayas had accepted that they wouldn't get paid together. But for her pride's sake she decided now that she wanted to know her sister's secret.

"Tell me what the zhooniyaa is for, or I am leaving our fish camp. Going back to Mama."

The light was a deep and mysterious shade of blue and the water had pink edges. The waves were gentle and the fish, no doubt, were swimming close to shore, right into their net. Omakayas was surprised to see, in her sister's eyes, a glint of amusement. Surprised, and then angry!

Angeline had no right to laugh at her little sister, no right to keep a secret that wasn't much of a secret at all! No matter what she did for Angeline, it seemed, she was never her sister's equal.

"Gigawaabamin, I'll be seeing you!"

Omakayas spoke firmly, and then, with a hop as broad as her namesake's, she was gone into the woods. She knew that she could run swiftly, and also that Angeline wouldn't leave the dried fish behind. So what if the net was heavy? So what if Angeline couldn't pull it in herself? So what if Angeline had to stay there all night and guard her little fish camp and smoking fish on racks? Omakayas fairly flew toward the fragrant stew that Yellow Kettle surely had warming over the fire. She hurried toward the sight of her grandmother and mother and her baby brother. The only good thing about working with Angeline was that she hadn't had to put up with Pinch.

Omakayas heard voices as she ran. She stopped and sneaked forward. The voices were coming from a low clump of bushes. As she got nearer to their source there was no mistaking the bossy voice of her cousin Two Strike. Omakayas couldn't make out all of the words, but Two Strike was yelling out one of her rousing, angry speeches. Omakayas jumped into the clearing and saw that several boys surrounded her, among them, both Pinch and the Angry One.

"Ahau!" Surprised, they were all silent, Two Strike included. As the silence went on and on, and they just stared at one another, Omakayas had an odd feeling. They were waiting for her to leave! A confused hurt clogged her chest, and for a moment she was speechless. Her face heated up. She didn't know what to say, or do. Two Strike was muscular, lean as a fox, her face set in a snarl. The boys were intent, disturbed, almost guilty-looking.

"Why don't you go away, back to your woman's work," Two Strike said.

If Omakayas hadn't just done a hard day's unappreciated work, and felt an angry frustration with her sister, she might have walked off. But Two Strike's arrogance, ever since she killed the moose, was worse and worse.

"Women's work is hard!" Omakayas yelled.

"Oh?" Two Strike sneered and struck a warrior's pose, fists on her hips. "Shall we see who's tougher?"

Omakayas had to fight back, even though she knew she wasn't as strong as Two Strike. If it came to a contest of strength, she would lose. Two Strike was meaner and better at fighting. Omakayas had already decided that

114

when it came right down to it she couldn't hope to beat Two Strike that way. No, there had to be another way. She stalled.

"You'd better run away," laughed Two Strike.

"I won't," Omakayas answered, and held her ground.

"No? You dare to say no?" Two Strike sauntered close. Her muscles were hard as iron bars, and her belt held two skinning knives. Her bow, as usual, was around her neck and a full quiver of perfect arrows decorated her back. A shooting contest was out of the question, too. The only option Omakayas could think of in which she might stand a chance was running.

"I'll race you," she said simply.

"Too easy," laughed Two Strike.

"Fine," said Omakayas. She had a way out now and seized it. "Then catch me!" Whirling, she darted off into the brush, and for a few bounds she imagined that Two Strike had actually taken her up on the challenge. When she realized that no one was behind her, and when she stopped, and heard no footsteps behind her, only laughter, she quit. She began to walk, her face burning now with embarrassment. After a while, she was aware of footsteps. She turned, imagining that Two Strike had either thought better of her mean words or reconsidered her offer to race. But no, it was the Angry One. He caught up with her and walked alongside. Suddenly, he spoke.

"She's trying to start up a war party with the little boys

as her warriors. They want to go against the Bwaanag. It's stupid."

Omakayas suddenly felt much, much better. She could breathe easily. Her eyes did not sting. Her throat didn't pinch. She had thought that he was part of Two Strike's war gang. Before she could even stop to think why she felt so much better, he jumped out ahead of her.

"Maybe Two Strike is scared to race you, but I'm not!"

They both started running. At first it was only a pretend race. Then, as Omakayas drew even and then slightly ahead of the boy, he speeded up and raced her in earnest. They were both swift runners, and flew down the path so evenly matched, so intent, that they ran straight into the clearing around the cabin and startled Bizheens. He was propped next to a tree in his cradle board, playing with some pinecones and a little piece of maple sugar tied to the head guard. He was so surprised by their sudden appearance that he started to cry. With a swoop, Omakayas was with him, comforting him, patting his tiny face, and cajoling him into a tearful smile. As usual, she tried to make him laugh but, failing that, she managed to soothe him and comfort him until he pressed his face into the curve of her neck and sighed away his last little sobs. The Angry One watched her efforts and Omakayas smiled at him over the baby's head. He smiled back, then frowned, looked around quickly. He's checking to see if anyone saw the frown drop off his face, thought Omakayas. The Angry One seemed relieved to find nobody was watching him and soon he backed away, stepped out of the clearing, and left, melting off down the path.

THE SWEAT LODGE

After Omakayas and her family moved into the cedar cabin, close to town, where they would live all winter, they cleaned and set up their winter sweat lodge. The lodge was a tough frame of curved young branches. It was set just a little behind the cabin and it looked like a nest placed upside down upon the ground. In the center, a pit was dug to receive hot stones, the asiniig, the grandfathers. When water and healing medicines were placed on the hot stones, a healing steam hissed up and filled the little lodge. Everyone had a job that would contribute to the maintenance of the lodge, for the lodge kept them healthy in the winter, and clean, and when they used it the spirits heard their prayers.

Omakayas was required to pick and clean the cedar with which she would carefully line the earth floor. It was Pinch's job to gather the right kind of asiniig for the sweat lodge. Every morning, Yellow Kettle shushed his grumbling and sent him out to the place near the point of the island where he could pick those rocks from the beach. He was supposed to gather the firewood, too, but for days he'd skipped out very early, before dawn, to range the shores with Two Strike.

"Where is that boy?" Yellow Kettle was exasperated. There were fewer and fewer days in which to prepare for winter, and everyone's help was important. There was a low growl of irritation in her voice. Angeline raised her eyebrows at Omakayas, and they exchanged a look that said "Let's not bother her!" Omakayas took the copper pail to the side of the lake, to fetch water, and quietly set about stoking the outside cooking fire.

"He hasn't gathered any wood! He should be helping clean the house! I have to keep this fire going hot today! Where is he!" Yellow Kettle muttered as she poked at yesterday's stew. Omakayas hoped she'd dip some out and eat it up, quickly, in order to improve her morning outlook. Nokomis put a twig broom in her hands and together they swept out the floor of the cabin. They continued outside, sweeping the debris of leaves, twigs, dried mud, and burnt bits of charcoal away from their cabin. Nokomis brought out the blankets and they hung them in the trees to air. They would beat the dust out, keep the blankets in the sun for days to make sure they were clean and free of lice. Both Nokomis and Yellow Kettle were very fussy about keeping everything around them neat. There was a place in the cabin for everything that they used. Pegs in the wall for coats. Iron hooks for the stew pots hung near the little fireplace. Antlers over the door held Deydey's precious gun. There were shelves built into the wall to store boxes of medicine and even their blankets. Stretched beaver skins and otter skins hung on hoops along the sides of the wall. Everything had to be put back into its place before the family went to bed every night. Omakayas loved the little cabin. She never wanted to leave it. They would never be able to build a cabin this neat and snug anywhere else. Mama's irritated voice broke her thoughts. "That Pinch is supposed to help clean the sweat lodge! Gather the wood!"

Yellow Kettle was holding Bizheens. The baby was so plump now that he wore little ankle rings of fat and his arms were creased and dimpled. His round cheeks glowed. Mama fed him tiny bits of meat that she chewed for him until it was very soft, then pressed into his mouth. Luckily, Bizheens was good at melting her anger. He ate eagerly, smiling at his new mother with an alert interest. Bizheens loved Yellow Kettle and was not in the least intimidated by her moods. After she finished feeding him, the baby watched Yellow Kettle with amused interest as she stomped around the cabin. When she hoisted him onto her back, in his tikinagun, the jerky anger of her movements only made him smile. He grinned so happily up into the tops of the trees that Omakayas almost thought he might laugh. But no, he was distracted by Andeg's appearance as the crow floated near for his morning scraps. Omakayas fed her bird quickly and then ducked back into the cabin.

Four great bearskins, hunted two summers ago by

Deydey and Old Tallow, made the sleeping area on one side. She rolled these up to bring them outside to shake. Omakayas's doll had its own bed, too, next to hers. She had woven a small sleeping mat and pieced together a blanket from clothing scraps. Omakayas tidied up her doll's bed, too, and smoothed its clothes down. She tucked her doll into its tikinagun. Then she brought in the eight trade blankets and the three made of woven rabbit skins and carefully piled them on top of new cedar boughs. The cabin filled with the sharp fragrance of the cedar. Omakayas set down the water and then took more of the cedar that Nokomis had cut and spread it across the floor of the sleeping area. Everyone slept on top of the fresh, blessed cedar for softness, to ensure good dreams, and because it smelled good every time someone moved and it was crushed.

At last, Pinch appeared.

"Oh, so you're back!"

Mama's eyes lighted on her son, returning dirty with sticks and leaves in his hair, not the slightest bit embarrassed to find everyone else at work so early.

"Eya', ningah," he said in a cheerful voice. "What's to eat?"

Fortunately for Pinch, his new little brother had succeeded in softening his mother's mood. Yellow Kettle was just stern—not furious anymore. Knowing that he was lucky, he set to work gathering and hauling wood. He worked for a while picking up kindling and pulled big branches home from the woods. He was eager to use Deydey's ax to cut a branch into burnable lengths. Deydey had taught him carefully how not to chop his own leg, but still, Mama sent Omakayas out to supervise him in his work and make certain he didn't have another accident. Pinch had a small, messy pile of wood cut by the time Two Strike came looking for him.

The girl strode into the clearing like she owned it and frowned.

"Izhadah. Let's go," she ordered him, abruptly, just as Yellow Kettle came around the corner.

"I'll say when to go," Yellow Kettle told her niece. Omakayas was busy helping Pinch heap his pile high, and she turned to see Two Strike glaring at her mother.

"He's coming with me," said Two Strike imperiously. She was carrying a short lance, decorated with seagull feathers, and this she thrust into the ground. "He's needed for the war party!"

Now, there were times that Omakayas felt angry at her mother, times that Yellow Kettle put her to work when she wanted to play, or times when Omakayas thought she was short-tempered and unfair. But that didn't mean Two Strike had any right to insult her mother! Yellow Kettle didn't think so either. When Two Strike put her lance in the ground, Yellow Kettle froze in place, as though to contain her immediate wrath. She seemed to get bigger, taller, and then she hardened like rock. Omakayas immediately shrank back. Pinch dropped his mouth open, then winced and kept his face screwed up. Even Bizheens stirred a bit and his little brow furrowed. Yellow Kettle continued to grow, and harden, bigger and bigger. That was when Omakayas realized that when her mother was mad in times past, she hadn't been really mad. In fact, Omakayas saw that she had never really known her mother mad, even at Pinch. For when she became angry with Two Strike now, she was really angry.

There was no explosion, there was no thunder, there were no words, only power. It was as though a great wind simply picked up Two Strike, disarmed her, and placed her underneath Yellow Kettle's arm. Even with Bizheens on her back, Yellow Kettle carried Two Strike as easily as a stick of wood.

"Where are you going with me! Put me down!"

Two Strike, enraged, began to struggle as Yellow Kettle walked down the trail with her. She might have tried to strike out or even bite, her fury was so deep and uncontrollable, but just at that moment Deydey appeared, Angeline at his side, and when he saw Two Strike tucked underneath the arm of his wife he knew that something serious was happening. He joined her, spoke for a moment. Then, amazingly, Two Strike seemed to fly through the air and land beneath the arm of Deydey. Like a bear, with one flip of her arm, Yellow Kettle had transferred the rebellious Two Strike to her husband. He now carried Two Strike, and the four of them, counting an interested baby still tied onto Yellow Kettle's back, walked quickly down the trail to Auntie Muskrat's.

As her mother and father disappeared with Two Strike, a great feeling of happiness washed over Omakayas. Her heart was still hot over the scorn that Two Strike showered on her. The killing of the moose had permanently changed her cousin for the worse. Finally, something would be done! Two Strike would learn her lesson. Nokomis now emerged from deep in the woods, carrying a load of fresh cedar. Omakayas told her what had happened, then asked what would happen to Two Strike. She couldn't help but ask eagerly, which made Nokomis pause.

"You would like to see your cousin punished."

"She deserves it, nookoo!"

"Ganabaj, maybe. Or perhaps the Gizhe Manidoo has something else in mind for her. Come sit down with me, my girl."

Omakayas sat down next to her grandma and helped her to clean the cedar, taking off the dead and rough pieces, and tie together the boughs to made a nice firm springy mattress. "Two Strike has an unusual destiny," said Nokomis, "we have been watching her. We think it could go either way."

Omakayas didn't grasp the meaning of what her grandma said, but she could tell that Nokomis was carefully choosing her words.

"She has her grandfather's spirit, and as you know, he was a grand warrior and an excellent negotiator, who secured this island for us and made certain of our trading partners. She has his fire, but she is young, and she lacks his ability to focus the flame. She needs guidance. Her family will put her out alone in order for her spirits to find her."

"But it's cold," said Omakayas, startled. When children fasted, it was usually in the first warmth of spring, just before the flies and mosquitoes hatched. At this time of year, there was hard frost on the ground.

"They will send her with a blanket," was all that Nokomis would say.

Omakayas nodded, kept her thoughts to herself. Now was the perfect time to speak, to surrender her secret, to tell her grandma about the dream that clearly said she should go out into the woods and fast alone. Her spirits were still looking for her! She knew it, but she didn't want to hear it. She stuffed the dream and message back inside of herself and continued to work on the cedar, breathing in its comforting pungence. In spite of herself, she felt a little sorry for Two Strike.

Perhaps as a result of not telling her grandmother about her dream, that night Omakayas dreamed again, more insistently. She saw herself standing on a piece of bark, streaking along the water. Her face was marked with black charcoal. There was an island in the distance. The piece of bark went faster and faster until she knew that if she moved the slightest muscle she would fall from it and drown. Before her, she sensed a great, dark shadow.

I've had enough of this, she thought, waking up, still dizzy from the speed of her bark boat, sweating from fear, and worried about the shadow of the future.

EIGHT

THE TRADER'S

Omakayas and Angeline had come to trade. They were always welcome at the trader's, for their family was well respected. Hardworking basket makers, quill workers, hunters, fishers, strong portagers, medicine gatherers, master jeemaan builders, and intelligent chess players were related to Omakayas. Still, although the girls were extremely proud of the two bales of dried fish, the result of their work, they stood shyly in the trading store doorway, smelling the spicy air. Finally they gathered the courage to walk in. They set their heavy fish bales on the counter and looked around.

A barrel of salt sat plump and round on the floor and

a tin of something called pepper stood behind the counter. There were two small casks of molasses, a wooden box filled with cakes of sugar high on a shelf. Bolts of fabric—red and blue trade cloth, calico with the tiniest flowers and leaves on it—ribbons of every color, tools, and bullets filled the counters and shelves. There were sweet-smelling medicines in small beautiful bottles. Peppermint. Cloves. Myrrh. Angeline sounded out the black marks on the labels.

"What have we here?" said the trader as he came through the little back door. Seeing the two girls, he smiled and leaned back on his heels, folding his hands over his round belly. Angeline suddenly became very shy and pointed at the fish.

The trader lugged the fish bales over to his scale, weighed them, and then tested a piece of one of the fish with the end of his knife. He nodded and then took a long flat fork and wiggled it into the middle of the bale. He drew out a morsel of fish and with a shrewd look at Angeline he popped the sample into his mouth. He chewed. The girls held their breaths. His eyes lit up.

"Excellent quality!" he said. He wrote down a number on a piece of paper, and now Angeline shook away her bashful air. She took the paper in her hand and regarded the number. She mouthed the chimookoman number to herself to be sure, then frowned. Politely but firmly, she took the pencil from the hand of the trader,

127

and slowly constructed another number.

"Oho! Sharp dealings from these pretty girls!"

The trader crowed, delighted to have the chance to barter. He tapped his chin with the greasy pencil, wiggled his eyebrows up and down, and wrote down yet another number. Reading it, Angeline impatiently shook her head, and tapped on the number she had written. The trader heaved a sigh and wrote down yet another number. This number made Angeline bite her lips and narrow her eyes. She hesitated, took the pencil, and carefully wrote down still another number.

At last, at this number, the trader nodded and stuck out his hand.

"Howah!" Omakayas almost shouted with pleasure. It was exciting to see her sister behave so strongly, and with such purpose. Now, with the credit that their baled fish brought, they looked at the items in the store with new eyes. The spools of ribbon, the loops of brilliant glass beads, the fabrics and the candy, all were available to them. They had a rich, substantial feeling.

"Little sister," said Angeline, "you thought that I was working to buy a gift for Fishtail. You were right. But here is something you don't know. I was also working to buy something for you. Little sister, you need a new dress. Look at the one you are wearing!"

Omakayas hadn't really thought about it, but now, as she looked down at the trade cloth dress she'd been washing

out and wearing all year, she saw that it had tiny holes in it from eager raspberry picking. It was stained and mended, faded on the front and hem. She was surprised to see how old it looked next to the new material in the store! How happy she was to pick out fresh new cloth. She looked for a long time at the blue, but it was too much like the dress she had. She considered the yellow, but then changed her mind and with a firm nod settled on the red. Angeline had it cut, and then bought white beads for trim. She also bought brilliant beads and enough expensive black velvet for a vest she would make for Fishtail.

Omakayas wanted to ask whether the vest would be a wedding vest, but she didn't dare spoil the good feeling between them. Angeline might frown and close up if she said too much. So she helped Angeline pick out little things—tobacco for Deydey, hanks of beads for Mama and Nokomis, black licorice candy for Pinch. Angeline didn't know what to buy for Bizheens, but finally settled on a bell that would hang on the head guard of his tikinagun. Every time he batted the bell, it would reward him with a musical tinkle.

As they walked away from the trader's, bearing their happy gifts, they were silent in thought. Finally, Angeline spoke.

"Do you think he will come home?" she asked carefully, her voice working hard to control the hope and fear in her heart. Immediately, Omakayas knew exactly the "he" whom her sister meant.

"Of course he will!" Omakayas exclaimed. It had not even entered her mind that Fishtail might not return. There were dangers, of course, but she knew that he was strong and clever.

"When he comes home, you'll set up your lodge," she

teased, "and in no time I'll be an auntie."

Taken by surprise, Angeline laughed. Then she threw her blanket shawl over her shoulder and hugged her little sister. With Angeline's arm around her, as they walked down the road, Omakayas felt completely warm and protected. They passed the school where, soon, Angeline would go once again to learn to scratch out the tracks that spoke. Writing, she called it, ozhibee'igay. Now that it was clear that those chimookomanag memory tracks could not be trusted, Deydey was anxious for his daughters to unlock their mystery. Maybe Omakayas would learn the speaking tracks that winter. Maybe she would go to the school as well. Angeline kept her arm around her little sister's shoulder even when they came to the rough parts of the road. They grabbed each other's shawls and joked and laughed as they carefully picked their way through the mud and garbage left out by the chimookomanag.

"It's because they live in the same place all the time," said Angeline. "Their garbage piles up. If they moved the way we do all summer, it wouldn't be so bad."

There was that difference, too, in the way these chimookomanag lived. Omakayas and her family moved to maple sugar camp in the spring, then to their birchbark house near their gardens, then to fish camp in early summer, then often out to a berry-picking camp and always to a ricing camp. It was true, the garbage didn't have a chance to pile up. Besides, they didn't throw out the same things that the chimookomanag found useless. Even now, Omakayas's foot kicked up a little omooday, a tiny glass bottle with a piece of paper pasted on it. The paper was tracked with words that Angeline read.

"Tinc . . . tincture. I don't know what that is. Of peppermint. I don't know what that is either."

"Some kind of mashkiki?"

"Let's keep it and ask the Break-Apart Girl."

Angeline liked the Break-Apart Girl too, and wanted to visit. They drew near to her house, but she was nowhere in sight. They lingered just outside the gate, peering in at the amusing gookoosh and trying to coax the silly chickens to them. Finally their friend looked out an upstairs window and waved. Moments later, she burst out the door and ran toward them. Laughing, she threw her arms around Omakayas, who hugged her back. Omakayas pointed toward the cabins and by using signs told her that they had moved into town. The Break-Apart Girl clapped her hands together, then put her finger to her nose to signal a beak. She was asking about Andeg. Omakayas pointed south. For two days now, she had not seen her friend, nor any other crow on the island.

The Break-Apart Girl was so friendly, so good to them. Surely she did not want them to leave! Omakayas wanted to ask her why the others, the big chimookomanag, wanted her people to go off into dangerous territory, but the idea was too complicated to get across by signs. As always, walking along, the Break-Apart Girl brought out a treat from her apron pocket. This time it was a kind of chimookoman bread that was made with something sour in it. The bread was chewy, soft, delicious. The girls munched slowly as they walked toward the beach and when they got there, as always, they bared their feet and stretched their toes in the sand. It was a warm fall afternoon and the water was perfect. All summer, the sun had heated the lake and it took a long time to cool off, so the water was warmer than the air, and even warmer than it was in the beginning of the summer. With a daring look, the Break-Apart Girl pointed at the remotest part of the beach. She took off running.

Holding their parcels carefully, Omakayas and Angeline followed. When they caught up with her they set their parcels in a safe place and took off their dresses and put them neatly with the parcels. The Break-Apart Girl took off her dress, too, but kept on some clothing of a trimmed white stuff. Omakayas wanted to see how the clothing was made, but it would be rude to look too closely. She couldn't help notice, though, that along with the dress the Break-Apart Girl had shed a stiff, short garment that had fit around her waist, pinching it tight. Without this thing, the Break-Apart Girl was shaped just like any girl and she seemed happy to run and play, to dive into the water. She couldn't swim, but she could throw herself under, she could splash, and she could chase

Omakayas and Angeline up and down the sandy shallows and lie in the warmth and stare at the clouds.

THE BLACK GOWN

After they had dried off, arranged their hair, and said good-bye to their friend, Omakayas and Angeline walked through the town of LaPointe to the black gown's praying house. The Catholic black gown, Father Baraga, insisted that the Catholic Indians decorate the inside of their praying house with flowers and cloth. The girls wanted to peek inside, for they'd heard it was a pretty sight. Standing on her tiptoes, her hands cupped to the glass of the window, Omakayas peered into the quiet room. There were ribbons draping the walls, it was true. Big fancy arrangements of ribbons and flowers decked the table in front of the praying house. On the wall, the two sticks of wood, nailed together, that Angeline called a cross were surrounded with glittering balls of some substance that Omakayas had never seen before. She tried to get a better look, strained forward, stood taller. Suddenly, as though lifted by a wind, she was hoisted into the air by a pair of strong hands!

It was Father Baraga himself, lifting her closer.

"Peendigen!" He invited. He spoke the language of the Anishinabeg and although the words stuck in his mouth as though he carried a pebble under his tongue, Angeline and Omakayas understood most of what he said. He wanted them to enter this beautiful praying house and listen to his God, or Manidoo.

"Meegwech, meegwech," they said, thanking him as they backed away. They didn't really want to go inside. Father Baraga's face was grim even when he smiled, and he was something of an awesome and forbidding sight. In that black robe, for which he was known, he stalked the streets of LaPointe looking for people to join in his praying house, and he ranged far and wide visiting Anishinabeg in their camps. Father Baraga made Omakayas uncomfortable, and she was glad that her family clung to their own ways. Although they were not interested in his white God, however, Deydey respected the hardy priest. He liked that the priest had troubled to learn their language and could speak so well with them.

"Aneendi g'deydey?" Father Baraga asked the girls. He wanted to know where their father was. He spoke to them for a while. The girls easily understood that Father Baraga wanted Mikwam to come visit the church and see the special decorations. They told the priest that their father was hunting, and that when he returned they would give him the message. Then they both felt a huge well of laughter bubbling up inside. There was no reason for the laughter, but it almost overtook them. Before they embarrassed themselves, they said good-bye and ran swiftly off.

The next day, the Break-Apart Girl came walking up to the cabin with a basket on one arm. She was wearing a long blanket cut and sewed in an interesting way. The blanket flowed down, over her shoulders, to the end of her majigoode. It covered her break-apart waist, which Omakayas now knew was terribly pinched in by the odd garment she wore underneath. On her head, the girl wore a small cloth bucket. Everyone exclaimed at it. Nokomis brought her in and sat her down in the corner of the cabin. The girl took her head bucket off and gave it to Nokomis to examine. After Nokomis looked it over, she approved the stitching.

"If you put a bottom on it, you could use it to carry things too," she said. "It could be useful!"

The Break-Apart Girl had no idea what Nokomis said, of course, but she smiled with all her teeth showing. Then she took the cloth covering off the things she had in the basket. There were two small bags of flour and another of salted pork, which was very good to fry with fish. The girl pushed these things at Nokomis, who thanked her profusely. Everyone sat together, without speaking, unable to communicate any better than to smile and nod from time to time. After a while, Omakayas grew tired of this, and gestured for the Break-Apart Girl to come outdoors with them.

The women of the family were preparing for a sweat bath, and Omakayas and Angeline invited the Break-Apart Girl to join them. Old Tallow had already prepared the huge fire with the stones in it. The stones, asiniig, or grandfathers, were nearly ready to be placed inside the lodge. They were red-hot and glowing in the big fire. It was time to bring in the bucket of water and sing the right songs. Omakayas gestured to the Break-Apart Girl to walk with her to fetch water, which she did willingly. Everything else was ready when they got back. Old Tallow was already inside, and also Nokomis. Yellow Kettle was outside, tending to the fire. Angeline slipped off her dress easily, and showed the girl how to crawl into the doorway.

"Ombay," she called, very cheerfully, from inside.

The Break-Apart Girl seemed frozen, rooted to the ground, and drew away, smiling faintly, when Omakayas pulled at her blanket coat.

"Come in," she said, "you will feel better. This is good for you." But although Omakayas smiled in as friendly a way as possible, and took off her clothes in a laughing way and tried to make the chimookoman girl comfortable, the Break-Apart Girl was clearly embarrassed. With many a wave, she turned and walked swiftly down the path into town.

And so, together, the women proceeded to enjoy themselves. When the door was closed, they sang and prayed. Nokomis placed pinches of fragrant tobacco on the glowing rocks and spilled a dipper of water on them. The cleansing steam filled their lungs. When it got so hot inside that Omakayas couldn't stand it, Old Tallow raised the skin flap on the doorway. They breathed the cool outside air for a while, and then, using two big antlers, Yellow Kettle picked more rocks out of the fire and brought them into the lodge. Again the flap was closed, and the medicine, good smelling cedar tips, was sprinkled on the rocks. Dippersful of water were poured out and the steam rose again. The women usually brought the grandfather rocks in four times and prayed in each direction. Afterward, they let the rocks cool slowly and ate a bowl of rice and berries, cleaned up the lodge, let the outside fire burn down. Night had come, and now the fire glowed in darkness. Soon there was a pure and peaceful moonrise.

As the older women talked together just outside the lodge, Omakayas made herself very quiet. She curled on the fragrant cedar where the hot stones still emitted a gentle warmth. She kept her ears open, although she shut her eyes and pretended to sleep. It was the best way to hear things the women thought too grown up for her ears. She heard Two Strike's name.

"Ii'ii, Two Strike . . . is our Little Frog asleep?"

"Looks like she's sleeping."

"We had a time with her, that child."

Nokomis was talking, for it was she who had been called upon to spend time with Two Strike.

"She listened," said Nokomis, "but did she hear? I don't know."

"Her father was never strict with her after her mother died, and Muskrat has her hands full with LaPautre."

Omakayas didn't have to open her eye even a slit to see that Nokomis made the quick fist-to-mouth sign for drinking the ishkodewaaboo, the water that burned. Albert had developed a love for the stuff that disarranged men's minds. Deydey rarely took any of it, for he said that the burning water was a false spirit.

"Muskrat said her troubles with Two Strike were much less before Albert took the ishkodewaaboo. Anyhow, we put her out to fast."

"Where at?"

"The little northwest island. We wanted her to stay out there. Not run away!"

"That was a good idea," Old Tallow laughed.

"If she's going to be a leader, an ogitchidakwe," Nokomis said, "she needs to listen to her elders. She can't go around talking back and stirring up the little boys all the time!"

"At the same time," said Yellow Kettle, "you don't want to kill her spirit. I've had to be careful, too, with my Omakayas."

Omakayas kept her eyes smoothly shut and breathed evenly, although her heart raced. She could almost feel Yellow Kettle's eyes upon her, checking to make sure she was still asleep.

"Our girl might seem dreamy, but she very definitely has a gift. I'm sure of it. Nokomis, you told me."

"Geget sa," agreed Nokomis, "she has a deep spirit. Omakayas can tell me the medicines, too, as we walk in the woods. She knows so many of them already, I'm amazed at her knowledge. Sometimes I think she is told how these medicines work by the creator, as well, for I am surprised at what she says."

"I'm surprised too," said Angeline, "by how much she can remember!"

Not as surprised as Omakayas, who almost sat up in amazement at the praise from her big sister.

"The one I feel sorry for is Twilight," Angeline went on. "She has lots of extra work to do. That boy who lives at their house, the son of the old man, he does help out although he always looks like he just bit into a green walnut!"

The women laughed a bit. "You're right," said Yellow Kettle, "you never see that boy smile. He's glaring all the time. But he lost so many it's no wonder."

"Maybe that is why the old Miskobines is so good-hearted."

"You value life then."

The women agreed, as did Omakayas, silently, in her heart.

"Ii'ii," said Nokomis, "we'll bring Two Strike back tomorrow. We'll see how she did, if she got some help out there. If she won't listen to her elders, at least she'd better listen to the spirits!"

Omakayas felt a fuzzy, comfortable warmth stealing up along her limbs now, and her head felt very heavy on her blanket, on the ground. Fire flickered on the insides of her eyelids. She tried to keep listening. But the voices of the women blurred. The cozy warmth invaded her and soon she was drifting softly into her dreams.

NINE

TWO STRIKE'S WAR

Two Strike Girl was not in the least upset by the spirits, nor was her fire put out by hunger and loneliness. She returned as tough and braggy as ever, saying that nothing could affect her, and that the spirits had not wished to change her direction with any particular vision or dream. Two Strike still defied Auntie Muskrat and wormed her way out of every task she was given, so poor Twilight had to haul twice as much water, work twice as hard at setting fishing nets. Even Little Bee complained of the way her older cousin treated her, bossing her around, making her pick up after her and bring her food as though she was a chief. After eating, Two Strike ran away from Auntie

Muskrat's every morning, and remained stubbornly in the woods making plans for war.

But who was she going to fight?

The Bwaanag, who terrified Albert LaPautre, lived far across the water and inland. There was no way that Two Strike and her war party of boys could paddle over and find the Bwaanag, even if they were to steal a canoe. They hadn't the weapons, either, though they labored hard to put together an arsenal of bows and arrows, sticks, rocks, and even a broken old musket that had for a time been used as the handle of a digging hoe. They had no enemy to fight, though they sewed together a hand made of tattered old buckskin and painted it with stolen vermilion. A red skin hand, stuffed, was the signal to go to war. Every day, they practiced war behavior—sneaking, ambushing, killing, yelling cries that paralyzed their invisible foes, and, most of all, returning triumphant. At last, though, they tired of all the pretending and Two Strike chose an enemy close to hand, an enemy that offered her a grave insult.

One night, Pinch told Omakayas about it.

"Sister," he whispered, late, after the flames of the fire had turned to coals, "I may never see you again, for tomorrow I do battle."

Omakayas was half asleep. Groggily, she rolled over. "What?"

"Ssshhh, my sister, this may be good-bye."

Omakayas woke up entirely, worried by her brother's

strange mood. She wiggled closer to him, whispered that she was listening. With some relief, he went on, speaking gloomily, as though he was a doomed warrior.

"The enemy finally showed itself to Two Strike yesterday, and tomorrow, at dawn, she means to attack."

"What happened, brother? You must tell me!"

"One of Old Tallow's dogs, the black one I think, growled at Two Strike. Besides, she never got a puppy, remember? Two Strike has sent the red skin hand to all the boys. At dawn we are to attack their village and wipe them out."

"Whose village?"

"The village of the dogs."

"Do you want to go?" Omakayas could hardly believe that her brother would want to, or dare, attack Old Tallow's close companions.

"Are you crazy?" said Pinch, his voice trembled a little. "Of course not. That's why I'm telling you this. Old Tallow will beat us with a big stick if we hurt any of her dogs. I just don't know how to get out of it!"

"Let me help you," said Omakayas, her brain working quickly. Together then, whispering in the dark, they concocted a plan. When they finished with the plan, Pinch gave a great yawn.

"I knew you would help me, my sister," he said, and with that he turned over and began to lightly snore. Omakayas sighed. Her bed was warm and soft, but she couldn't sleep, for the rest was up to her. Stealthily, she sneaked from her bed, stepped quietly around her parents' sleeping forms. Of course, it was impossible. Deydey's hand shot out and grabbed her ankle.

"Deydey," she said, crouching down, "I have to . . ."

"Let her go," said Mama sleepily.

He turned over and Omakayas quickly slipped out the door into the dark.

Omakayas didn't mind going outside at night. Deydey had told her frightful stories of grandfather owl, and spirits with mischievous intentions lurked everywhere, but she also believed that there were comforting spirits at work. There were rustles, hoots, calls from unseen sources— some unsettling, some beautiful and musical. Sometimes balls of light glowed, or radiant green spots littered the ground. During the day these were ordinary-looking lichens and mushrooms, but during the night they gave off a ghostly fire. They were the food of the dead, but they were also strangely beautiful. By the time Omakayas reached Old Tallow's cabin, however, she was frightened, for she'd got to the scariest part—waking Old Tallow from her sleep.

But that proved easy, for of course the dogs barked long before Omakayas arrived. They heard her approaching and told Old Tallow, who was still awake. Even though the night was far advanced, she was working on something at an outdoor fire. She had a small kettle heated by white-hot coals, and she was concentrating by the light of a small pitch torch.

"Ahneen!" Omakayas greeted Old Tallow from some distance.

"Ombay," said Old Tallow, inviting her near.

"Ahneen ezhichigeyan?"

"Making this pipe stem, this okij," said Old Tallow, proud of her work. She was concentrating on the perfection of the details she was adding. She was so intent on the art of her pipe stem that she'd probably lost track of time. The wood was a beautiful dark color, and she had carved a striking pattern into it, then melted lead into the grooves. The lead hardened and made the design on the okij. Old Tallow frowned at her work, adjusted it a bit, and didn't ask why Omakayas was visiting her at such an unusual hour. Old Tallow had no curiosity about such things.

"Don't you wonder why I'm here?" asked Omakayas.

Old Tallow glanced out of one fierce, skeptical eye, but said nothing.

"I'll tell you then," said Omakayas. "Pinch is in trouble. Two Strike wants to make war, and she has Pinch in her war party. But he doesn't want to."

Old Tallow said nothing.

"He can't get out of it, for if he did, the others would laugh at him. But he doesn't want to go on the war party!"

Still, Old Tallow maintained her silence, squinting

hard at the flames. Omakayas reached the end of her patience.

"Don't you want to know who they're attacking? They are making war on your dogs!"

At this, of course, it was as though a sudden rod stiffened Old Tallow's spine. She sat bolt upright in outrage, stared hard at Omakayas, and then she laughed. Her laugh startled Omakayas. It started low in her throat, like a sifting of sand on the shore, and then it burst out in a crash. Omakayas jumped.

"At dawn," she told Old Tallow. "They will make their war at dawn!"

The sand sifted away and Old Tallow stopped laughing, spoke.

"I won't give away your brother, but I'll be ready for Two Strike's war party. Now crawl into my bed and go to sleep, little one. Stay here, and that way you'll see the fun!"

Several hours later, Omakayas woke in Old Tallow's bed, a snarl of blankets and skins like the den of a bear woman. Gray light was just beginning to lift in the arms of the trees. Omakayas found a crack in the chinking of the logs, and peeked into the edge of the woodpile, where Old Tallow's dogs lived in the neat lean-to houses that Old Tallow built for them. Their houses were much more nicely kept and better built than Old Tallow's own. Her cabin was stuffed to the brim with every conceivable kind of junk she'd ever acquired or traded for—old brass pails were loaded with crumpled furs, the floor was covered with piled bolts of cloth, with sheaves of bark and equipment for hunting, ricing, sugaring, and for just being Old Tallow. The cabin smelled of old leather and rank new raw animal hides, and Omakayas was glad that the chink in the wall also let through a little fresh air.

Suddenly, one of the dogs pricked up its ears. Omakayas watched as the next and the next dog became alert and looked with steady dog anticipation toward the place where, Omakayas was sure, the little war party would appear. Two Strike knew that Old Tallow tied her dogs up at night. Shooting at them with their bows and stoning them with their rocks was easy work. Or so it would have been if Old Tallow had really tied them. For Omakayas now saw that first one dog and then the next stepped beyond the boundary of its rope. There was no rope! When the warriors burst into the yard, instead of tied-up dogs to torment, there were a pack of alert and suspicious free dogs who didn't like the arrows in the bows or the stones in the children's hands.

Two Strike gave the first yell, and rushed forward. The dogs stepped back, for they never before had been attacked by humans and couldn't quite believe that these small ones would want to hurt them. But the warriors, seeing the dogs' hesitation, grew bolder and threw their rocks. The rocks hit the dogs with solid thunks, but not one of them whimpered or ran. They seemed intent on figuring out their next move. Omakayas's throat pinched. The dogs were puzzled by the sudden viciousness directed toward them. They had always been loyal to humans, their troubled stance seemed to say, why should the humans turn on them now? What had they done?

The warriors released the first volley of arrows. Omakayas held her breath. Luckily, none of the arrows hit. Suddenly, from behind the warriors, there sounded a strange, thrilling cry that stopped the children in their tracks. Even Two Strike glanced around to see what made this sound—the sound of a furious lynx combined with the screech of an owl. When the thing that made the sound slowly rose out of the bushes, half the warriors dropped their weapons. For Old Tallow had sneaked behind them and now reared before them mighty as a tree, her eyes flashing and her crooked grin wide. She advanced toward them thrashing a great, stout stick rhythmically and whirling a set of whistling pliable sticks in the air above her head. She threw the stick down before her, bounded forward and crouched.

The wands whistled and snapped with terrifying cheer around the heads of the war party. The warriors turned to race past the dogs, but now, at word from their master, the dogs leaped from their houses and circled the children, grabbing and pulling back any warrior who tried to break from the circle.

"Throw down your weapons, every one of you," Old Tallow said.

Even Two Strike dropped her bow and war club, though the sneer never left her face. Her warriors stood ashamed and foolish, heads bowed, as Old Tallow informed them the purpose to which she had cut the willow withes in her hands, the ones that cut through the air.

"Every one of you will come forward and bravely endure, as warriors must, the punishment of captives," said Old Tallow. With that, she proceeded to methodically pick out of the circle one warrior after another. She gave each one a switching with the stinging sticks and made that warrior howl or in silent shame wonder what came next. When she came to Pinch, Omakayas didn't know what to hope. If Old Tallow spared him, Pinch would be outcast from the group. Two Strike would know he had betrayed their plan, and she would get even in ways that made the switching seem a light punishment. On the other hand, a switching from Old Tallow was nothing to take lightly.

Pinch looked aware of this, and frightened, as he left the circle. Sure enough, Old Tallow raised the switches, struck once, twice, three times. Pinch began to cry. Tears popped from his eyes but he was too proud to make a sound.

"Oho! We have a brave little warrior here, do we?" Old Tallow growled. "I have ways of making you beg for mercy. I will tie you up." Old Tallow tied Pinch up with a few quick motions. He looked aghast at the rope that bound him. Perhaps he thought she'd eat him. "I'll put you in my house," said Old Tallow, to the horror of the other warriors. "What these ones get will be a mere taste of what you will endure!"

"Gaween!" cried Pinch. But all the same Old Tallow hoisted the bound boy on her shoulder, carried him to the door of her cabin, rolled him in.

Even Two Strike seemed subdued by the severity of

what Pinch would endure, and she tried to struggle forward, although the black dog held the seat of her pants.

"Take me!" she cried out. "I am the head warrior. I began this war party to avenge an insult from your dogs. If one of my warriors is captured, I will be captured too. Take me! Let him go!"

Again Two Strike tried to step forward, offering herself. Omakayas couldn't help but admire her spirit even as she hated her, and perhaps Old Tallow felt the same way, but she expressed it harshly.

"You are indeed a leader, and your offer is a leader's offer. You will receive twice the punishment of your warriors, but I will keep Pinch and do with him as I like!"

With that, Old Tallow gave a terrible switching to Two Strike, who endured it, however, with contempt and walked back to her warriors giving not even a backward glance to the powerful old woman who had beaten her in her first war.

After Old Tallow had given a talk to the war party and then sent them off into the woods, feet dragging, heads bowed, Omakayas began to work Pinch's rope loose. She shushed the whimpers he could not help emitting when he thought of his fate. "She won't hurt you, silly," said Omakayas, removing the rope. "Old Tallow just gave you a gift. Your war party will think you the bravest of all. You'll have to make up a story about what she did to you. But she is glad you alerted her because, after all, if she had gone off in the morning as she often does, or even run from her cabin too late, Two Strike could have killed one of her dogs. And if that had happened . . ."

"Oh," said Pinch, his voice shook, "oh, don't even think about it."

The two traveled home when the sun was up and pretended that they'd both got up early, very early, in order to set out snares for rabbits and check the ones from the night before. And although Yellow Kettle glanced suspiciously at Pinch, who hated rising early, and although later on it was observed all through the camps that the boys were unnaturally quiet, and Two Strike too, the war was over. No one knew of it, except those involved. Old Tallow's justice was rough, but quick. Even her dogs forgave the warriors when they crept back, later on, and threw them bits of stolen meat or pieces of their own bannock. For when they were cured of the war fever, the boys regretted having hurt the dogs who would, after all, have defended any one of them to the death. They knew very well that the dogs were loyal to all people whom Old Tallow told them to love. Before the war party members had skulked home, Old Tallow had told her dogs, in the warriors' hearing, that it was their duty to stay devoted even to these cruel children who had betrayed their trust. These words had shamed them all so bitterly that even Two Strike's fire was put out.

BIBOON

WINTER

TEN

OLD TALLOW'S COAT

Deydey always said that the winter could not truly begin until Old Tallow donned her coat. Hers was a coat of strange magnificence, a patchwork of destroyed fabrics and new furs. Each year, Old Tallow added something new to the coat so that it never diminished, only increased in complexity. There were lynx and marten furs, velvets, parts of blankets, rabbit, bear, and otter scraps as well as trade wool. There were even other coats contained within the coat, as if it had swallowed them up. Old Tallow reworked her coat every fall to keep the stitching tight. She added inside pockets or loops of belt for her knives, a holster for her hatchet, a hood one year, an extra collar.

One cold, blustery afternoon, as Omakayas hurried back from a trip to Auntie Muskrat's, where she had been visiting Twilight, she saw Old Tallow bounding through the woods. She was wearing the coat. It was a thrilling sight. The furs and patterns billowed around her and her dogs loped beside in chase of some invisible prey. They passed quickly over the frozen earth and were gone. Omakayas kept walking, the sight fresh in her mind. Sure enough, by the time she was in sight of the cabin, the sky went a frigid white and the air filled with flakes of snow. The snow fell deep that night and did not melt in the morning. Winter had definitely arrived.

The long winter nights were for storytelling, and Nokomis was known as an excellent storyteller. To request an aadizookaan, or story, someone gave her a small amount of tobacco, just enough for her to smoke in her pipe. Nokomis took the tobacco and sometimes she smoked her little pipe as she thought about the story she would tell. When the wind howled outside and Omakayas was safe in her rabbit-skin blanket, curled tight against Nokomis, there was nothing better than to hear Nokomis begin a story. She told the holy stories and the funny stories, the aadizookaanag that explained how the world came into being, how it continued to be made. These stories explained how people came about, and how humans learned so much from the wise and hilarious teacher,

Nanabozho. This last being, who did so many absurd and yet meaningful things, was a favorite of Omakayas. Another favorite story, though it chilled her and sent Pinch crawling for Mama's lap, was of that terrible monster of the ice and snow, the wiindigoo. When Nokomis told a wiindigoo tale, her voice deepened and even the wind outside quieted down to listen. Her eyes grew narrow and a cold breath sighed through the cabin walls. Omakayas pulled her blanket close around her, shivered deliciously, and listened.

THE LITTLE GIRL AND THE WIINDIGOO

This happened in the old days, said Nokomis, when some people had great powers and the animals spoke to us. In those days, there was a little girl whose mother died. Her people were unkind and they did not take care of her. She was considered the smallest one and made of the poorest stuff. She never got the fat meat, only the bones from the bottom of the pot of soup. She never got the warm spot, next to the fire, but shivered beyond its circle. Nor was she given good clothing to wear, but made do with the tattered ends of skins and worn-out furs that other people threw away. Yet, because her makazinan were full of holes, someone took pity on her. Some spirit looked her way and was moved to watch out for her.

One of the old men began to say that a wiindigoo must be about. The kettles were moving on the fire. Wind came from nowhere. The flames died and yet the water boiled. An owl was caught within a rabbit's snare. Now, for sure, the old man said, let us make ready. A wiindigoo is coming near.

Here is how we will do it, the old man told the people that night. We will all come around the fire and we will all try to smoke this pipe. Anyone who can get it to light without a match will be the one with the strength to fight the wiindigoo.

The warriors tried first. One and then the next took that old man's pipe and worked on it, breathing on it and begging it to light all by itself. But nothing happened. Each of the old men tried next, and found that they, too, were useless. The women tried, both the old women and the young. No matter how they talked to the pipe and blew into it, still nothing. At last the children tried, even the babies. There was no success.

Then the old man said that there was one person too humble to try the pipe. This person was sitting at the edge of the fire, where she always sat, and she was wearing the raggediest clothing. She didn't even own a blanket. She was that poor. The people turned around. At first they were so used to overlooking the girl that they saw no one. Then all of a sudden they noticed her. And some of them laughed. Some of them said it was no use, why even bother. They told the old man to forget about it. But he insisted, saying that even the lowliest must try now or they would all be devoured.

So the little girl was brought near the fire, though she was shy, and so afraid that she could not look at anyone who helped her. Feeling the warmth of the flames for the first time, she thought how nice it felt. Her heart grew stronger. She was able to take the pipe in her hands. But only when a woman felt sorry for the girl and put her own blanket around her shoulders, did the girl dare to put the pipe to her lips.

The first time she breathed on the pipe nothing happened. Some people shook their heads in disgust and went away. The second time she breathed on the pipe it remained cold. More people left and others said that there was no hope. The third time the girl tried to light the pipe without a match, nothing happened, again, and she almost put the pipe down from shame. But then the spirit who was looking after her spoke so that only she could hear. Think of your mother, said the spirit, and the girl thought of her mother. She touched the pipe and it caught on fire.

Now she knew exactly what she needed to do. She suddenly became very powerful. First she called the old man's dogs to her. They came and sat directly at her feet. Then she instructed the men to find her two stout rods of sumac. They should cut them and bring them to her at once. The women, she said, must use the fire she had started to boil a great kettle full of tallow, and not be afraid of her when she started to grow.

Soon it became very cold. Everything began to crack. They could hear the trees bursting in the woods, even the rocks. The people saw the wiindigoo stride across the lake, which froze beneath his feet. He was made all of ice, a huge man-shaped thing white as frost. He came on land and wherever he stepped ice took over. The cold got worse. It filled the girl, too, and she started to grow. She grew into a giant, and then she faced the wiindigoo.

First she sent the old man's dogs to kill the wiindigoo's dog. They did so easily. Then she took the rods made out of sumac in her hands. When she did this, they turned to copper.

With the first rod she knocked down the wiindigoo and held him. It was a terrible, raging battle, but finally, with the other rod, she killed him. Then she drank a cup of the tallow soup from the kettle on the fire. Instantly, she came down to her own size again. The dogs became regular dogs when she let them lick some tallow from her hand. She then opened the mouth of the dead wiindigoo, which was full of jagged teeth made of ice. Into this creature she poured the rest of the boiling hot tallow. The ice melted off the wiindigoo entirely, and when it did, a normal man was left lying by the fire.

This man was never told he had been a wiindigoo, but he was watched very carefully. He was told that he must hunt for the little girl. So she had everything she wanted from then on.

Now, said the spirit who protected her, you must always help these people. Even though they scorned you, they will now respect you. You must show them how to be more human.

Eventually, the little girl married and was happy. She had four children, and when she was old she told this story. And when the people heard it they all agreed it was important to be kind to the ones most helpless—the poor, the old, the children. You never know whom the spirits have chosen to help you and even to save you. The smallest and poorest-looking person might have enough power to kill a wiindigoo. Mi'iw minik.

While he listened to Nokomis's aadizookaan, Deydey always worked to fashion something with his hands. He made three kinds of snowshoes—the curved snowshoe, the little round bear-paw snowshoe, and the snowshoe with a tail. He used the split soaked basswood he had collected in the summer, and moose guts for the lacings, as fresh as possible. He sewed tight webs of sinew between the sides of the snowshoe hoops. Deydey made drums, too, for use during ceremonies. He made another, special drum, which he planned to give Fishtail when he returned. He carved a pipe in the shape of the claw of an eagle holding an egg. He carved a pipe stem that twisted in a beautiful whirl. He made lacrosse sticks, fishing decoys, a doll's cradle board for Omakayas, a toy rattle for Bizheens. He made snow snakes, carving them with beautiful designs. These snow snakes were the favorites of Pinch.

Every afternoon, Pinch took his snow snakes and went out to the edge of the lake with the other boys and Two Strike. There, they took turns seeing who could throw the snake the farthest across the ice. They conducted endless snow snake contests and wars. First one and then the other was champion of the snow snakes. When they tired of that game, they went sliding farther down the shore where the land sloped excitingly to the lake. If they got going fast enough on a piece of elm or birchbark, they'd slide far onto the ice. Of course, they made this into a contest too. The one who slid farthest was declared chief, or ogitchida. Two Strike coveted the title, but more often it was the Angry One who threw himself farther on the ice.

Omakayas often went sliding with her cousins and sometimes, if the snow was soft, they had long snowball wars that lasted into the afternoons, broke off at dusk, resumed the next morning, and went on for days. One day, when the snow was just right, Omakayas ran to Auntie Muskrat's to fetch her cousins. The Angry One was there, hauling water up from the inlet where the family kept a great hole open in the ice. Today, he wore the same forbidding look that Omakayas was familiar with on the face of Old Tallow. For some reason, maybe because the day was so bright and the world so cheerful, the angry frown made Omakayas laugh.

"What's so funny?" growled the boy.

"You never smile."

"Don't feel like it," he grumped. "I want to beat Pinch

at snow snakes today, not haul water."

"Go on, then," said Omakayas, feeling kindly toward him, maybe because he was so absurdly mad. "I'll haul the next few loads of water."

"You will?"

The Angry One looked completely astounded at her offer. He stood rooted to the icy ground, so surprised he was almost upset. Omakayas took the brass trade pails from his hands, dumped the water in the big kettle, or akik, steaming on the outside fire. Then without another word she went down to the inlet where the hole was chopped in the ice, leaving the Angry One still mystified. Omakayas laughed to herself as she filled the pails. He probably wonders why anyone would do anything to help such a sour person, she thought, and he's right! It's worth it, though, just to see the surprise on his face!

That day, the winter snow snake games and sliding turned into the biggest snowball battle ever conducted. Of course, Two Strike was the leader of the boys, and Pinch was her top warrior. Omakayas was the leader of the girls, and Twilight and Little Bee fought fiercely at her side. But the boys, including some cousins from the village, outnumbered them. They were being driven from their territory, farther and farther into the woods. Two Strike's snowballs were hard, often carrying rocks. Once, she hit Omakayas full in the face. Omakayas was stunned. The smack of the snowball and the pain of the rock were awful. She was too proud to cry. Little Bee got hit next, and she did start to cry. Suddenly, from nowhere, with a blood-curdling shriek, the Angry One leaped into the battle on their side.

His arms moved so fast they blurred. He packed snowballs hard, too, and always hit whoever he aimed for. He got Two Strike right on the nose, and she was so surprised that she plopped down right on her seat. From the snowy ground, she peered up at him, wiping the snow off her face.

"Ombay, my warriors, let's fight to the death!" she yelled, leaping to her feet. But Pinch had already started to laugh at his snowball-fight chief, and once a warrior laughs there is no going forward with the fight. To the disappointment of Two Strike, everyone was suddenly friends. For the rest of the day they constructed a dog sled and tried to train Makataywazi and Twilight's dog to pull it—but the two always bounded after waaboozoog or pulled in opposite directions. They were hopeless. The children finally headed back to their homes, to the warm stew pot and the snug fur robes, to the fragrant cedar of their sleeping corners. Only as Omakayas approached her cabin did her thoughts turn, as they always did after a few hours of distraction, to worry over the fate of the men who went to the four directions, and those who were on the journey to the west. No word had come from them yet.

LEARNING THE TRACKS

Every morning now, Angeline and Omakayas set out for school. Once they arrived at the schoolhouse, they shook the snow off their makazinan and slipped into their places in the school room. A cast-iron stove at the back of the room threw so much heat that they preferred to sit up front. It was easier there to study the marks that the teacher made on the big black piece of slate, and to copy them onto their own smaller slates. They saw the Break-Apart Girl every day now, and could even say her name, Clarissa, though it still sounded like Gisina. She passed out the slates every morning and began the lesson by writing out the alphabet on the main blackboard. The small slates that the girls used had to be returned before they left, as well as the pieces of chalk that made the fascinating marks. All morning, Angeline and Omakayas practiced letters and numbers. In the afternoon, they went home. As they walked back to the cabin, the air around Omakayas's head seemed written with swirling figures and

patterns. She had tried so hard to make sense of all the teacher said that she couldn't shake the marks out of her head.

Soon, she knew all of the letters, and the sounds of the letters, and she could say them along with Angeline. At night, sometimes, they practiced the letters by tracing them in the frost that formed on the inside of the cabin walls. They taught Deydey the letters, and he took their teaching very seriously. Every night, he practiced writing the letters that composed his name, Mikwam. When he could write out the entire alphabet, he asked his daughters the sounds of the letters. He learned the sounds of the letters along with them, and they practiced so much that Yellow Kettle grew annoyed and said, "Stop those strange noises! Let's have a story! Anything, to drown you out!"

SETTING SNARES

The winter day began with a strange blast of sunlight, then dripping water and an odd, surprising warmth. Everyone walked outdoors hardly bothering to grab their blankets or winter leg wraps. The sudden visit of summer, a blue sky and snow melting in the trees, sent people out to fish and hunt. Old Tallow took her dogs and ventured to the wildest part of the island, hoping to bring down a deer. Deydey and Pinch went out to the inlet to chop fishing holes in the ice. As for Omakayas, she went out with her grandmother to set snares in places where the rabbits ran. Wearing their round bear-paw snowshoes, they tramped through brush in the pleasant warmth of the midwinter sun. Just past the place where their garden sprouted in summer, there was a clearing where lightning had struck a stand of big trees, bringing some to earth and burning others. Here, Nokomis sought many of her medicines. It was also a place with heavy new growth of tender-barked trees, and lots of cover for rabbits.

Omakayas looked carefully at the ground, reading the long oval tracks of the waaboozoog. They took certain paths through the undergrowth. As she followed the path of the waaboozoog, Omakayas had to see the rabbit itself in her mind's eye. That was the trick to catching it. She had to imagine just where it would jump, just where it would nibble, just where it would stop. It was the jumping that was most important when it came to setting the snare. Omakayas bent a pliable branch over to the earth, and attached to it a noose made of sinew. If the rabbit jumped exactly where she thought it would, the loop of sinew would catch it and the branch would snap up, holding the rabbit out of the reach of foxes. As she carefully set each loop, Omakayas frowned in concentration. This was delicate work. Nokomis was very good at it. For every snare that Omakayas managed to set, Nokomis set five or six of them. And then, often, she would go back over Omakayas's work and make tiny adjustments.

As they worked, Omakayas noticed that her fingers, which had not even needed mitts on the way out, were getting numb with cold. Sighing, she took the mitts she'd had stashed in her waist band and shoved her hands deep into their warmth. So much for that teasing taste of summer! Next, she noticed that her feet were freezing, even in her fur-lined winter makazinan. She stamped her feet and moved quickly. The cold was sharper now, and penetrating. Nokomis's eyes were flashing in this cold. She loved being outside, whatever the weather, picking medicines or setting snares. "That's all the summer that we'll get!" she cried. It was very cold now. "Let's start for home!"

They almost didn't make it.

The snow had melted on top, but now froze so quickly that there was a tough crust of ice on top of every drift. When they left the shelter of the fallen brush and tried to walk along the shore, they slipped and slid. They tried walking the way they'd come, through brush. The snow was still slippery on top, but somewhat better. But the cold was becoming deadly. Their breath, which had shown in the air as steam, now froze instantly to the sides of their blanket hoods. Bits of ice came down their brows. Nokomis said, "We can't stop moving." Her voice was harsh as a raven's call of alarm. Omakayas jolted awake. She felt sleepy, and she knew that was dangerous. They had worked up a sweat setting so many snares. The cold had fallen so suddenly that, should they stop, their sweat could freeze on their bodies and draw out all of their inner warmth. A sudden drop of cold like this could kill them.

"Watch your step!" Nokomis's voice was even louder and boomed in Omakayas's ears. She knew that her grandmother saw that she was getting clumsy. It was the cold. She couldn't feel the ends of her toes, then her whole toes.

Her feet burned and then she couldn't feel them, either.

"Keep walking!" Nokomis shook her, and Omakayas knew that it was a shake of desperation, meant to save her. She couldn't speak though. Her mouth was sealed by the drowsiness, her tongue was cold. The ice drops hung heavy on her eyelids. Plus it was so much trouble to talk. Omakayas longed to lie down in the snow and sleep. One part of her mind knew that was certain death. She could not consider it. The other part of her mind could not help dwelling on how pleasant it would be.

"Omakayas!"

She had fallen. Nokomis pulled her up and shook her harder now. Omakayas came awake and smiled at her grandmother. "I'm coming," she said obediently. On numb legs she stepped and stepped. One foot moved, and then the other. She kept track of them. They amused her, down on the ends of her body. Her feet moved in and out of her line of vision. She almost laughed, but the laugh froze inside of her. Sleeping was the only possibility. "I'll just sleep for a minute," she heard herself telling Nokomis.

The next thing she knew, she was being jounced along on her grandmother's back. The old woman staggered beneath Omakayas, and had trouble moving at all, for their combined weight drove her snowshoes down below the crust of ice. When the crust broke, Nokomis wallowed in the snow. Several times, she had to put Omakayas down and hoist her up again, onto her back. At last, just as she wondered if she could do it again, Nokomis saw Deydey picking his way toward them. He'd gotten worried about them and followed their tracks into the woods. Once he got to them, he grabbed Omakayas and then he and Nokomis tramped as quickly as they could back to the cabin.

Her body wouldn't let go of the cold. Omakayas couldn't stop shaking. She shivered so hard that when she tried to focus her eyes, everything kept bouncing. Yellow Kettle's worried face blurred. Pinch's face, too, his mouth open in interested awe. She confused the face of Nokomis bending over her, so gentle and tough all at once, with Angeline's. Both wore masklike shadows. Even Bizheens, a round bundle in Mama's arms, seemed to tremble in the air. Deydey warmed the skins, wrapped them around her. He heated up rocks in the fire and set them, covered in furs, all around her body. How her toes and fingers itched and stung when the blood began to circulate back into them! Nokomis rubbed them with bear fat. Tears stung Omakayas's eyes, but she knew that she suffered frostbite, not freezing, and she would be all right. Still, the cold had sunk right to her very center and took a long time, all night in fact, before the tender care of her family could transform it to warmth.

When she woke, Omakayas felt completely recovered. Her feet and fingers were swollen and tender, but they all had feeling. She saw Nokomis sitting above her with a makak in her hands, and a spoon carved from a piece of horn. The spoon dipped. A thin and delicious soup poured between her lips. The warmth going down drove the last bit of cold from her center, where it was lodged tight.

"The cold surprised us all," Nokomis told her.

"Is everybody home now?"

Omakayas was deeply impressed by the power of the cold. It had reached into her with phenomenal swiftness, and taken hold of her warm life with no warning. The embrace of cold was painful at first, then beautiful and comforting. The cold told her that all she had to do was lie down and sleep. The cold had beckoned her to a death of deceptive ease.

Nokomis busied herself at the fire, stirring the soup. Again, Omakayas asked, this time with fear.

"Is everybody home?"

"No," said Nokomis. "Your Deydey is out looking for Old Tallow. She did not return from hunting. One of her dogs came back last night and threw itself at our door, barking and whining. Deydey followed the red dog immediately."

Omakayas's heart lurched. Had the cold found and taken Old Tallow? The answer was not long in coming.

The pale sun had just reached over the low pines, into the oiled paper of the window, when Nokomis, Yellow Kettle, Angeline, and even Pinch ran out the door.

Makataywazi had barked at the approach of Old Tallow's dogs, and soon Deydey lurched into the clearing, dragging a hastily constructed sled. Old Tallow was tied onto it. Omakayas crawled to the door. As the great old woman was lifted off and brought into the house, it was impossible to tell whether she was alive or dead.

They laid her on blankets and furs, as close to the fire as they could put her without scorching her. Nokomis pulled the pile of patched coat away from Old Tallow's chest, and put her ear to the old woman's heart. "She's alive!" Hearing that, Omakayas crept back into the covers. If anyone could survive the grip of cold, Old Tallow could, and if anyone could help her, Nokomis and Mama would do the job. They worked quickly. Mama took the water that was heating on the fire and added snow so that it would not be too hot. Nokomis bathed Old Tallow's face, hands, and feet in the warm water. Taking off the shawl that bound her hat onto her head, they found one side bloody. Apparently, she'd been knocked unconscious. They boiled cedar into a tea and dribbled it slowly between her lips. And they spoke to her, over and over, in voices they would use for a child.

Abruptly, Old Tallow sat up, knocking the makuk of tea from Mama's hands.

"Ishtay!" Nokomis was overjoyed.

"Wegonen! What!" Old Tallow glared around her with all the gratitude of a trapped wolf. "What are you doing to me?" Then she frowned at her left hand and shook it like a great paw. "Can't feel it," she said abruptly, then fell back in a sudden fainting swoon.

"She's out cold again," said Yellow Kettle, but her voice was pleased.

"Maybe it's for the best," said Nokomis, her voice relieved also. "It's the only way she'll let us fix her!"

For sure, Old Tallow would live. Not only that, she was still herself—cranky, bold, irascible, tough. It was not until the next day, however, that she recovered enough to tell everyone just what had happened to her out in the woods. Deydey had to tell part of it as well, for he had found her. Between the two of them, they put the story together.

THE GREAT LEAP INTO NOTHING

"I was tracking that big doe," said Old Tallow. "I'd seen her tracks for about a month, and now I was sure I had her. Little did I know, ahau! After that nice warm morning it began to get cold, then colder."

At this, Omakayas nodded, remembering well.

"My dogs and I got down to the remote edge across from the island of the bears, and we finally saw her. Geget sa! I could not believe it. She was no ordinary animal, but a *white* doe. Fat and beautiful. And it seemed to me, my friends, that she looked over her shoulder as though to say to me that I, Old Tallow, was chosen to hunt her. To take her. And then I really wanted to catch that deer."

Nokomis gasped. "A white doe? A spirit animal!"

"Geget sa. That's right," said Old Tallow. "Right there, I should have put down my tobacco. I should have given her an offering for showing herself to me. Then I should have left her alone. But you know Old Tallow! I'm a hunter! I could not let her go!"

"So you started after her," Omakayas breathed.

"I did, my child, and let this warn you. There was no way that I was going to get that doe. My heart was full of greed. I kept thinking how I'd walk back to camp carrying the white doe on my shoulders. We'd have a special feast. Its hide would be a marvel! Greed. That's what filled my thoughts."

"It got very cold," Nokomis said, "how far did you track her?"

"Too far!" said Old Tallow. "Not that I got lost. Old Tallow never gets *lost*! But far enough so I began to feel a little tired. And then, the cold began to steal my brain. I saw the doe in front of me, so close. With the cold closing down on us, I started to chase her. I could not let up. That warmth made a mist once the cold hit. Soon, my dog and I got so close that we could see the doe just before us, moving through the fog and snow. Blending into its whiteness. We began to run. That's when she tricked us! My friends, I saw something no Anishinabeg will ever see. I saw the white doe walk into nothingness. Yes, she

stepped into misty air like it was solid. For her, it was. As for us, we tumbled off a steep cliff and down onto the rocks!"

"That's where Old Tallow must have hit her head," said Deydey, "for that is where I found her, nearly covered with the snow. And hear this. The tracks of that doe did lead to the edge of the cliff and then . . . nothing. Except a big mess of dog and human tracks where Old Tallow blundered and slid!"

Old Tallow laughed. "I sure made a mess going down all right. I fell a ways, then pitched ears over butt all the way to the bottom!"

Even Omakayas, who could see it all too clearly, had to laugh at the picture of Old Tallow in her big tattered coat

179

rolling and bouncing down the steep pitch of earth.

"And hear this," said Deydey, "her dogs saved her life. They must have talked it over, those dogs, for they sent only one dog back to fetch me. When I finally tracked them out there, here is what I saw. The other dogs were curled around Old Tallow for warmth. The whole pack saved her. If they hadn't lain against Old Tallow, she wouldn't have survived. Only that one hand," Deydey nicked his chin toward Old Tallow's hand, which was resting in a wooden bowl of warm water, "that one hand was out on her chest, with no mitten. I guess the dogs could not figure out how to cover it."

"I'm worried about that hand," said Nokomis. "That's why we're greasing it up. Can you get some feeling in it yet?"

Omakayas winced, remembering exactly how painfully the blood moved back into her fingers and toes. Old Tallow's face was neutral. She showed no hint of pain. "It's coming back, the feeling," she said, "just a few fingers are still numb."

Slowly, Nokomis nodded. She heated up more bear grease and gently painted it on the poor frozen skin. It was not good to rub the skin too hard, or heat it up too quickly. Everything must be done with the greatest delicacy, so as not to destroy more feeling. Slowly, with great care, she bound the hands of Old Tallow into great fur clubs and ordered her to sleep some more.

"Sleep is the best medicine sometimes," she said. "We'll

feed your dogs. Don't worry about anything, just sleep."

But Old Tallow had already gone into the land of dreams.

Old Tallow's hand was slow in getting better. Every day, once the fierce lady moved back to her own house, Nokomis took Omakayas along and went to visit. She changed the dressing, and examined the hand closely. As she did this, she taught Omakayas just how to do the same. All of this was part of her education as a healer. When patches of skin fell off, Nokomis showed her how to bathe the new skin in balsam water. Old Tallow now hobbled mightily since her toes were still painfully heal-ing. She didn't rest. Her dogs needed her, she said.

Most of her hand healed back, the skin new and red. Only one finger on Old Tallow's left hand still gave her trouble—it was the hand that was exposed all night. The last finger was not getting well. The winter moon turned from new to almost half. Slowly, worse and worse each time Nokomis and Omakayas visited, that finger was turning first a gray-blue and then black.

One day, Nokomis decided.

"You know what we have to do," she told Old Tallow. The woman slowly nodded, then shrugged as though to say, *I'm lucky anyway.* Omakayas looked at her grand-mother with incomprehension. Then Nokomis took out her small hatchet. Sitting on the pile of skins in Old

Tallow's cluttered little house, Nokomis began to file the hatchet on her sharpening stone.

"No!" said Omakayas.

Nokomis only shook her head, and gave her grand-daughter a special look that meant, *Hold on to your feelings, it's not you who has to lose a finger*! She kept sharpening the hatchet to a fine keenness, grinding it against the stone with a rhythm that would have been soothing had it not carried such an awful threat. The sound of the sharpening grated on Omakayas's nerves. She wanted to shout, to hold her grandmother back. Yet she knew that this was the only way to save the rest of Old Tallow's hand, and maybe even her life. For if the infection that killed her finger was allowed to spread into the rest of her body, the result would be deadly.

Nokomis built the fire up and put a stone in it to heat red-hot. She also heated the razor-sharp edge of her hatchet as hot as she could. "You will have to do these things," she said to Omkayas. "I want you to help." Omakayas watched and helped her with the heating of the metal. Old Tallow sat numbly in her chair, her face set in a snarl of unconcern.

"Now," said Nokomis, "you will help hold Old Tallow's arm still. She's so brave she wouldn't move it on purpose. Sometimes the hand will just react."

There was a cut log stump in Old Tallow's house that served as a chair. Nokomis poured boiling water on it and then put Old Tallow's hand down and spread apart the fingers. The fire blazed brightly, for light. Beads of sweat popped out on Nokomis's forehead, but they were not from the heat.

"Now put your hand on Old Tallow's wrist," commanded Nokomis. Omakayas did.

"Grip my wrist firmly," said Old Tallow to Omakayas, and then with her other hand she pointed to her eyes. "Look here. Keep your eyes on my face."

So Omakayas was looking straight into the strong old woman's eyes when her grandmother's keen hatchet fell. It was one swift, true blow. The metal lodged in the wood. Old Tallow's expression changed only in one slight degree—her mouth tightened on one side as though a stitch was suddenly pulled tight. As Nokomis pressed the wound to the heated, cleansing stone, Old Tallow's gaze became blazingly fierce and Omakayas saw one—just one—tear spring from the corner of the woman's eye.

Later, Omakayas had an odd thought. She wished she'd caught that tear. It was rare. Probably, it was the only tear Old Tallow had ever shed.

THE HEALING GIFT

"I want to use a piece of that moose hide we tanned," Omakayas told her mother.

"You mean Two Strike's special moose hide?" teased Yellow Kettle.

Omakayas didn't like to call it that. She wanted to make something very important, a gift, and that moose hide was one of the best she'd ever finished. She had thought long about her grandmother's teachings, the care she took in showing everything about her medicines to Omakayas. She understood that everything that Nokomis taught her how to do was involved, in some way or other, with healing and caring for others. Now, she wanted to help to complete the healing of Old Tallow, and she had an idea. She would make the old woman a pair of mitts that would cover the hand missing the last finger, and help to keep those hands warm. Omakayas could see the mittens in her mind's eye—big and bold, trimmed with otter fur, more beautiful than the ones that Old Tallow had lost. These mitts would remind her of the love that her family had for the old woman, who had helped them out and rescued them many times in the past.

That day, she and Nokomis cut the mittens out of the moose hide, and she began sewing them together with long pieces of sinew. She worked slowly, carefully, making each stitch count. She wanted Old Tallow to look at the mitts and understand that they would never come apart, or wear out, and that they would protect her hands forever. After the operation on the strong old woman's finger, Omakayas had been afraid that Old Tallow would not be the same. But the hand healed in remarkable time.

Although Old Tallow was not up to her usual course of hunting, not yet, she did accompany Nokomis to check the snares. She also helped Deydey and Pinch fish the holes in the ice, and pulled up large geegoonyag with her good hand, though she couldn't yet scale them or prepare them to eat.

The mittens would help. Omakayas smiled to herself as she worked on them through the day, into the night. She bent over them and sewed by the light of a bear grease lamp, squinting at the stitches, feeling her way along the soft, smoked hide.

ELEVEN

DEYDEY AND THE SOUL STEALER

When the snow was deep and there was enough fish caught to feed them all for at least half a turn of the moon, Deydey broke the winter's monotony by visiting with the stealer of souls. That was Old Tallow's name for Father Baraga. Omakayas always begged to come too, and he often let her accompany him to visit the priest. Deydey and Omakayas enjoyed Father Baraga's talk, for he did not adhere strictly to the insistent speech he used when he lectured in the praying house. Sometimes Father Baraga talked of the country where he was born, far off.

There, in a place called Europe, kings and queens ruled and great wars raged with terrible killing and many horses to carry the ogitchidaag. The black robe spoke of a country dotted with tiny fenced-off pieces of land where poor people kept gookooshag in their houses and slept in their gardens. He spoke of gichi-oodenan where huge numbers of people were concentrated, cities where the houses were made of stone and nobody moved from place to place, but stayed in one house all their lives.

Deydey had many questions about these places, and smoked his pipe on the ways of this world. He believed it when Father Baraga said that there were more chimooko-manag than the tongue could ever count. Some others did not believe such things, but Deydey said that he thought the priest spoke straight. The only thing that annoyed him about the priest was his behavior when they set up the medicine lodges. Baraga refused to go inside. Sometimes, speaking together, Deydey tried to persuade the priest that his own praying house or sweat lodge was just as good. The priest would not believe it.

One day, Deydey and Omakayas went to visit the priest, bringing him a bundle of dried fish. Father Baraga came out of his little cabin with a sleepy look on his face, rubbing his eyes. He showed them inside and rustled the papers at his table.

"I am writing down your language," he said.

He showed them the tracks. These written tracks formed a design that held the sounds of words—not just chimookoman but Ojibwe words. It was a marvel to them both that the signs his pen scratched out could be transformed into the things they said with their mouths.

"Will you teach this to me?" Deydey asked. Omakayas's heart pounded. She was on the trail of this learning, but she had written only white people sounds. She wanted to know how she could write words out of sounds in her own language.

"If you become baptized and allow me to baptize your little girl, I'll teach you," said Father Baraga.

"I'll have to think about that," Deydey said, regretfully patting Omakayas's hair. She felt good at his strong touch. Although she wanted to learn the scratching and the meanings of the marks, she was also glad. She would learn the secrets, but she wouldn't give her spirit in return. Her Deydey was careful and did not simply do everything the priest suggested. There were some who would do anything to please the priest in case his God happened to be powerful.

"Mikwam, the only way you can gain everlasting life is through my church," said Father Baraga.

His eyes were kind, almost pleading as though he was watching them suffer. He pitied them, she thought with surprise, and it almost made her laugh because they pitied him right back.

"Everlasting life," he said again, softly.

"Will my father, my mother, my grandfathers, and my grandmothers be there in this everlasting life?" asked Deydey.

"Were they baptized?" asked Father Baraga.

"No," said Deydey.

"Then they will not," the priest answered in a sad voice.

"Then of course I can't go," said Deydey, "I want to see them!"

Father Baraga only scratched his head, underneath his tiny useless cap, and sighed. There was nothing he could do about this family, nothing.

PINCH'S STRANGE FISH

It took a long time for Pinch to learn how to hold the fishing spear just right, balanced over the hole in the ice. It took him an even longer time to learn how to stay motionless. The last was hardest for Pinch, but he was learning from his new cousin, the Angry One. They two spent long hours at the fishing holes, sometimes not far from Deydey. They used the fish decoys that Deydey had carved and carefully balanced, so they floated just right in the water. With one hand, each boy moved the decoys so that they would wiggle just so. With the other hand, each held his spear. Over their heads they draped blankets so that they could see into the water and spear the moving fish.

All day, Pinch had caught only one tiny fish, while the Angry One and Deydey had filled a makuk each with fat mean-looking pike. Pinch brooded on his failure, and that night, as they sat near the fire after they had eaten the fish and praised their flavor, Pinch asked Deydey if he could make his own fish decoy to use the next day. Somehow he felt sure that if he made his own, he would attract fish and spear them with no trouble.

So Deydey took out wood, his carving knife, and some leads, which he heated up in a small metal can and would use to weight the fish carved of wood. All that night, and the next, Pinch worked on his fish decoy. He nicked his hands many times. He got frustrated with his poor carving. He poured a bit of hot lead on his foot and burned himself. All in all, it was a terrible task. But, at last, he completed his decoy.

As he showed it proudly to everyone, they tried not to laugh. It was the oddest shaped fish anyone had ever seen, with a fat lump on its head and a lopsided belly. One fin swam one way, one fin aimed the other. Pinch had rubbed a bit of red ocher into the sides for decorations. The spots were nothing ever seen on a fish before.

"We'll see how it works tomorrow," said Deydey, his mouth twitching as he looked meaningfully at Yellow Kettle. She put her hand on Pinch's frowzy head and told him she was very proud. But Omakayas saw that when Pinch held the fish up high and crowed, Mama had trouble holding back her laughter. It was a very strange, probably useless fish, for sure.

The next day the Angry One came by for Pinch and

the two started out for the fishing places. When he saw the decoy Pinch had carved, the Angry One put his lips together in a firm line and raised his eyebrows, but said nothing.

"Tonight, I'll have enough for a feast," Pinch declared.

"I'll keep the kettle ready," said Nokomis. She seemed to believe in him. "Ishtay, my grandson, you're becoming a mighty hunter!"

And Pinch walked proudly down the trail.

To everyone's complete shock, the fish that Pinch carved was apparently the most delicious-looking fish in the world. All the fish that lived underneath the ice wanted it. No sooner had he dropped it in than a big fish came hungrily with open mouth and Pinch speared it. Again, again. Deydey left his own fishing hole and came over to marvel. The odd-looking decoy fish worked every time.

THE GIFT

Omakayas wrapped Bizheens warmly and took him outside into a beautiful winter day. Behind the sweat lodge, underneath the pines, she had her own snow house. The walls were made with snowballs and chunks of ice. Omakayas took some jerky and bits of bannock bread. She hoped that Pinch had not yet found her snow house and wrecked it. When the two ducked under the soft fronds of winter pine, she saw that her house was still there, and she smiled with pleasure. Only a few snowballs were dislodged by wind.

"Neshkey," she said, jiggling her baby brother. "Our place is beautiful, isn't it?"

While she held him in her lap, she used her other hand to pat the snow into place. Bizheens watched all she did with shrewd eyes, approving of all her actions. She picked up some pinecones knocked down by snow and stuck them on top of the walls for decoration. Then she swept away the needles that had fallen on her snow house floor, and rested on her one chair, a flat rock around which she'd built the walls.

The beautiful arms of the pines reached down all around them, and the wind made a friendly rushing sound high in the needles. She could almost make out words.

"The pines are singing to us, baby brother," she said. "They are telling us Fishtail is all right."

Omakayas said this although in her heart, she didn't know if it was true or she just wanted to believe it was true. Bizheens looked up into the pine branches, as though he understood. He seemed to see something up there. He watched carefully, and then he burst into a babbling song that made Omakayas laugh. The shadows of the moving fronds moved back and forth over his happy face. Omakayas softened bits of bannock and jerky in her own mouth, then put them in his toothless mouth. Whenever he tasted something, his face always registered a look of comical concentration. Yellow Kettle said it was because a baby's taste is very sharp, and usually babies got nothing but mother's milk. Whatever the reason, the look was always hilarious and now Omakayas could not help but laugh out loud.

"Who's in there?"

It was the Angry One, come looking for Pinch, probably, to throw the snow snakes. Or maybe to fish. After all, he carried a long fishing spear on his back and the snow snakes in one chapped and mittenless hand.

"I live in here," Omakayas laughed. "Go away!"

"Sure," said the Angry One, and he actually did go away. Had she imagined his visit? Omakayas poked her head out and looked around. He was just about to vanish into the line of trees on the other side of the clearing.

"Come back!" she yelled. "I didn't mean it!"

The Angry One turned slightly and looked directly at the branches from which she was poking her head. He didn't seem to hear her. Then she surprised herself.

"What's your real name?" she yelled.

"Animikiins," he yelled back.

His name meant Little Thunder. While Omakayas was taking this in, he stepped away into the low brush and was gone.

Omakayas did not visit the snow house again for many days, but when she finally did, she found a gift. On the very end of her snow wall a little round stone had been placed. It was one of those rare finds that wash in from the deepest part of the lake. Sometimes, as though taking special care, the waves rolled these stones along the bottom until a perfect sphere was formed.

These stones contained protective spirits. She dropped it carefully from one palm to the other, her asin, her stone, and she thought about Little Thunder. He still didn't laugh much, or act foolish, or tease. That wasn't his way. But some of his sorrow and his anger was gone. He didn't look like steam was rising off the top of his head all of the time. He didn't always frown when people greeted him. Sometimes he smiled, and when he did, what burst from his face was the sunny look and pleasant spirit of the boy he'd been before his mother was killed.

The smooth asin rolled back and forth, back and forth. How many years had it lain underneath the waves?

TWELVE

THE MESSENGER

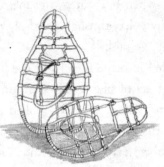

Omakayas was always to think back on the pair of bloody snowshoes propped up next to the door of their cabin. The blood was fresh, and it belonged to the messenger whose poor feet were raw with frostbite. He was a scrawny man, yellow-skinned and weak. It took a moment or two for Omakayas to recognize Cloud, who had left the island a strong and hearty young man. He sat in the warmest place before the fire and hungrily gulped hot soup. The grown-ups around him were very quiet, waiting. Soon more grown-ups arrived. The children were given soup and a roasted piece of weyass, but they were not allowed to talk at all. Nokomis sang the game of silence song to them low, and they listened hard for the words. The prizes were few, just a hastily made bow and some lumps of maple sugar obviously scared up for the emergency. Still, the children, including the boy cousins usually so exuberant nothing could persuade them to be quiet, did fall quiet and bundled together beyond the light of the fire. For when he'd eaten, the messenger began to talk in a scratchy voice, through painfully cracked lips.

"It is all lies," he said.

His words fell into the breaths of the listeners, woven together in a basket of silence. He went on.

"Brothers and sisters, we have looked to the east, we have looked to the south, to the west, to the north. None of the Anishinabeg has killed a chimookoman. We have not broken our treaty."

There was silence, a sigh of relief, and then grumbling. If the Anishinabeg had not broken the treaty, it meant that the chimookomanag had. The messenger went on. His face was pinched and desperate, his voice hoarse with pain.

"When the government tried to lure us out of our country by giving payments in the land of the Bwaanag, we went. Our Anishinabeg men waited at the place the land payments were supposed to be given out. Sandy Lake. Waited so long we became hungry, and hunted everything for miles around us. When that was gone, we talked of leaving, but the storehouse agent talked us into

196

staying. Not a one of us even spoke of breaking into that storehouse. But the agent, drinking the water that scorches the throat, ishkodewaaboo, destroyed the storehouse anyway and all around him! It burned to the ground one night!"

"Were the payments inside of it burned too?"

Yellow Kettle could not help but ask. She held her graceful arms around the tiny Bizheens, who cuddled close to her. In answer to her question, Cloud laughed. The sound of his laughter was awful, like the scratching of two rocks ground against each other. Omakayas put her hands up to her ears. It was a long time before the messenger spoke.

"We sifted through the ashes and found two coins. Exactly two. We gave ourselves the land payment then."

The messenger breathed hard, as though the talking had cost him all of his breath, but at last, with a deep sigh of pain, he spoke again.

"A boat arrived, filled with spoiled food. The boatman said that he was followed by the money and we must wait there for the good of our families. You can eat this, he said, dividing up the rations. Some did and some didn't. The meat was gookoosh, pork, and rotten. Maybe even poisoned. The flour was mainly worms and flour fleas. By then, however, some of our men were too sick to move on. Waiting had made them helpless. Those who couldn't move fell sick most quickly, followed by the men who stayed to take care of them. At last"—here Cloud's voice faltered. He sounded like a cracked piece of wood, his voice was no longer human—"I saw my brother die. My father. When I left, many were dead or nearly so and groaning for help. But the agents were gone. The boat was gone. Nothing was left. Nothing."

There was a loud moan, another and another, as people whose relatives had gone to see about the payments took in the terrible news. Omakayas was sitting near Angeline, who made no sound. She looked suddenly as though she was carved of stone. Her eyes stared straight into the black wall. Her lips moved faintly. Omakayas went to her, but Nokomis got their first and sat beside Angeline. Nokomis took her in her arms, let her sag hopelessly into the shape of a little girl.

"We don't know," said Deydey later.

Although he was shaken, he refused to declare Fishtail dead. He said they must be thoughtful, reserved. "Cloud is no liar. He speaks the truth. He saw with his own eyes what was happening. He saw most of the men dying, and knew he must return. But he did not see Fishtail die. He did not even see Fishtail sick."

"That is right," said Angeline, her voice firm, her lovely mouth held in a tough straight line. "I know in my heart he lives. I will pray he stays strong." But as she said these words her mouth trembled with fear she could not put aside. She crept into her blankets and later, in her sleep, Omakayas heard her sister whispering, as though she talked to her loved one in her dreams.

As for Omakayas, the next day and the next her heart was very heavy. She could not keep her thoughts strong. Every so often, when she thought of Fishtail suffering, tears came into her eyes and she ran to Bizheens. Omakayas decided that she would play with Bizheens all day and take care of him. Bizheens was the only one who would help her keep her heart hopeful. He had survived, after all, when everything looked impossible. The woman who had given Bizheens to Yellow Kettle said that he'd had nothing to eat for weeks but water, cedar tea, and a bit of rabbit soup. Yet, even without his mother's milk, he had lived. Though tiny at first he was now plump and cheerful and he knew how to play. Bizheens didn't know Fishtail and he didn't know that people could die. He didn't know that the agents of the government could lie and cheat. He didn't understand what had happened to him in his life. He only knew that he loved Omakayas.

THIRTEEN

THE WEDDING VEST

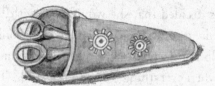

As though to show exactly how deeply she believed in the return of Fishtail, Angeline began work on the piece of black velvet she had bought at the trader's. First she cut out the vest with the precious pair of scissors that Yellow Kettle was so proud to own. Next, she beaded each of the pieces with a design she drew onto the velvet with a stick of chalk that the Break-Apart Girl had smuggled to her. The beading took a very long time, and it had to be perfect. Omakayas watched her pluck out beads that were hardly crooked at all. When she took apart one whole beaded flower, Omakayas thought maybe Angeline didn't want to finish the vest. Maybe as long as she worked on the vest she could believe in Fishtail's return.

The beads kept collecting. The flowers kept growing on the ends of beautiful twisting vines. The leaves were sewed on in beautiful ways. There were maple leaves, for the sugaring tree that they loved so much in spring. There were tiny twisting leaves of vines that grew on the edges of the woods. Omakayas marveled at her sister's work.

"I wish I could bead like you," she said, and she really meant it.

"Oh," said Angeline, dropping the pieces of velvet into her lap, "I don't know . . . do you think . . ."

Omakayas sat next to her sister.

"Don't be scared," she said, "he's all right."

Angeline's head drooped, her breath caught. Reports were coming in now, every week or so, of another man known to be dead. There were houses who had lost more than one of their men. People were packing up to move on, to live on the mainland with relatives, for the end of the winter was harsh. Angeline lived in fear of another messenger walking into their house with bad news. Every day that bad news didn't arrive, she fell asleep relieved. Every morning, she felt a new dread that the day would bring bad news. Now, she did something that surprised Omakayas so much she could hardly breathe.

"Here," said Angeline, holding out a piece of the velvet, "I want you to bead one of the flowers. I know you love Fishtail too, and he would be glad to know you helped with this vest."

Omakayas was stunned, even a little afraid, for two reasons. First, her sister was so nice to her that it frightened her. She was most often remote these days and regarded Omakayas as too small to bother with. Her sudden kindness made Omakayas think that Angeline might have sickened herself with worry. The other thing she was afraid of was messing up the beadwork.

"I'll show you," said Angeline. Omakayas sat down next to her. Angeline had made beading hoops out of split ash. The two hoops were carefully made, one just a tiny bit bigger than the next so that the material would be pulled snug when the top was set over the bottom. Then, in and out of the taut hoop with the material in between, Omakayas pulled her needle, securing bead after bead. Her hand shook when she started, and she was careful to select each bead to fit with the next. It took her all afternoon. When her flower was done, she showed it to Angeline, who scared her even more by saying it was very beautiful.

ZEEGWUN

SPRING

FOURTEEN

DEYDEY GUIDES
THE BLACK ROBE

"The Black Robe spoke with me. He asked me to show him the way to the camp of the far point people. He is hoping to grab a few more souls, I guess." Deydey laughed, but it was clear that he was planning to guide the priest to the place he wished to go.

"He doesn't know how to read the ice," Deydey continued, shaking his head. "This time of year, he'll step on a rotten patch! I better show him the way. You know, he has told me himself that he sometimes gets lost and wanders in circles."

"You should be here," grumped Yellow Kettle, "getting ready for the ice breakup and for the sugaring."

The trees were not yet ready to tap, and wouldn't be for a good amount of time. But snow was falling from the pine boughs. The bits of snow made soft little plopping noises when they hit the ground. Gradually, the winter was letting go. Still, Deydey knew that Yellow Kettle's reasons for objecting were different. He would only be gone a few sleeps there, a few back. Yet she would miss him. She didn't want him to go. Because she was Yellow Kettle, it was hard for her to say this. She was very brave, but she was worried, or maybe she had an inkling even then of what would happen to Deydey and Father Baraga. Maybe she saw ahead and read the danger.

THE LAKE SPLITS

Deep in the night, it began to complain. All day, the great booming sounds of the ice cracking came and went. Sounds traveled like gunshots from every side of the island. Everyone went down to stand onshore and watch. Of course, the whole family was worried about Deydey, but he knew the ice. Certainly, he would not get caught on the cracking surface. He would wait on the mainland, hire a canoe, and venture out until the water was open. Yellow Kettle sighed in irritation. Now it would be a little more time until he returned.

The children ran up and down the beach, following the loud reports, watching for a crashing collision of ice shards. On the shore, Auntie Muskrat stood beaming into the sweet blue sky, her hands on her round hips. With her stood Miskobines, the chief, Red Thunder. He had become like a grandfather to her children, and as his strength increased with every good meal Auntie Muskrat fed him, he had begun to use his skills in hunting and fishing to help the family. They were all dressed warmly and wore new makizanan.

Suddenly, from all the way out on the lake, a great black crack began. The children saw it and pointed in excitement. The crack traveled toward them fast as a moving snake. It came straight toward them, and when it hit the shore there was a vast and resounding *boom!* Auntie Muskrat and Miskobines were standing right where the crack hit shore. The force of the air that built up as the crack traveled struck them full force. They went flying right out of their blankets, backward into the sand!

Knocked over all of a sudden, they sat stunned. They shook their heads, addled, confused. Unhurt, they jumped up in excitement. Owah! Auntie Muskrat laughed hardest, describing the force of the wind that knocked them over. The lake was breaking. Things were changing. Spring was coming. The power of the world would show itself in new growth. All the animals would return.

THE DREAM

After Deydey was gone with Father Baraga for half the turn of the moon, Yellow Kettle said right out loud that she wondered where he was. When she said this, everything stopped. It was not the words that she said, but the sudden sound of distress in her voice. She knew just how long it took for him to get to the far point, and she also knew he should have been back before now. Together, once their fears were out in the open, the little family sat around the outside cooking fire and stared into the flames.

"Daga, n'gaa, smoke your pipe on this," Yellow Kettle asked Nokomis in a low voice.

Nokomis brought her pipe and then the family sat with her and they smoked it together, or touched the pipe, to show they were of one mind in their concern and prayers. Even Pinch was very quiet, his hands twisting. He didn't pull Omakayas's braid or even try to burn her foot with a hot stick. Angeline's heart was clearly stretched already from her worry about Fishtail, and she was close to shedding tears. Yellow Kettle breathed in tiny breaths and kept her eyes narrowed and her brow set. She had to keep up an angry and concentrated front, or it was clear she might cry too. As Nokomis passed the red stone pipe to her, the smoke carried their thoughts up into the sky to the great, kind spirit who showed pity to the Anishinabeg. Omakayas felt a sense of peace. No human hand touched her, but she felt as though someone infinitely kind laid a palm on her forehead.

She took a tiny puff of the sacred smoke and asked for her Deydey's safe return.

Maybe it was the pipe, or the heat of the flames. Maybe it was her fear, or perhaps it was the way her mind worked. Whatever it was, that night Omakayas dreamed:

She was balancing in the air. She was rising, then flying so quickly that the wind pulled at her clothes. Below, she saw the island where eagles made their nest. Omakayas's heart leaped. She recognized an island where Deydey often stopped to lay tobacco on the shore. He was there, sitting next to a black rock. In his hands, he held his long counting stick and his knife. He was about to put another cut in his stick, when she heard her mother's voice.

The dream was so real that as she halfway woke, while her eyes were still shut, she wasn't sure where she was. Then she heard her mother's voice outside the cabin, raised in annoyance. Omakayas opened her eyes. She was in her rabbit blanket, her feet toward the cold ashes of last night's fire. The morning had already begun.

When Omakayas stepped out of the lodge, her mother was jiggling Bizheens on her hip and glaring at the burnt stuff in the bottom of a kettle.

"Nobody notices anything around here but me! Why do I always have to be the one who remembers to take the pot off the fire!"

Yellow Kettle shoved the akik onto the ground in a fit of temper. Omakayas stepped back and stood beside the cabin. When her mother fell into a fury, it was best to let her rage all by herself, to fume and fuss into the wind. But it was too late. Yellow Kettle had seen her, and her frustrated eye caught sight of Omakayas's messy hair and dragging makazin ties.

"Is that my daughter with the sticky hair? Is Omakayas so full of important things to do she can't bend down and tie the makazinan, the ones I made for her? Aaarghuf!"

Poor Bizheens was jiggled so hard he shook all over. His plump cheeks shook and his solemn little face vibrated. If Yellow Kettle hadn't been so mad, the sight of him would have been comical. But right now the last thing Omakayas wanted to do was laugh. When Yellow Kettle's rage fixed on Omakayas, she knew that she should just stay still and let it roll like a loud but harmless storm high in the clouds. Yellow Kettle stamped, ranted, threw down the kettle, but always, at last, her anger blew out. She suddenly deflated. She sat down on the rock next to the fire and cried out for her husband.

"Where are you, my husband?" she asked in a still voice that sounded very young in the ears of Omakayas. Now she was safe to approach, and Omakayas did.

"N'gaa, I dreamed he was at the island where the migiziwag have their big nest. I dreamed he was sitting there, notching his counting stick."

"Aaaaaruf!"

Maybe she had spoken too soon. Maybe Yellow Kettle would say that it was foolish, just a dream, and that it should be disregarded. Nokomis, however, had come near while Omakayas was speaking and now she asked her granddaughter to repeat the dream. Omakayas told the dream as she had before.

"This girl has dreamed a dream," said Nokomis firmly. "Let's get men to go and look. The lake has broken. The two may be trapped on that island."

THE RESCUE

Miskobines was ready to go and look for Deydey. He wanted very much, in fact, to find this man whose family had been so good to him and to his people. The Angry One insisted he would go too, and his father agreed. Old Tallow wanted to go too. She took the canoe with the odd roof on the end, and Miskobines and Little Thunder took theirs. Miskobines had taught his boy to paddle expertly and told him how to read all things in the sky, the water, the earth.

The rescue party set off as soon as they had offered tobacco. They would trace their way to the island of the eagles—everyone knew about that island. It would take one day to get there and one to return. Not long, and the family would know one way or the other.

Those two days were the longest days of Omakayas's life.

Pinch was no help. As though he was jealous of people thinking of anybody but Pinch, he clung to Mama. Omakayas was disgusted and felt sorry for Yellow Kettle.

211

She had two babies—one to hold and one who tagged along begging for syrup or a little grease for his bannock. That last one had a runny nose and darting eyes. His hair poked every which way. His voice was loud and his demands were constant. It seemed to Omakayas that whenever there was a time of danger Pinch turned back into a baby. Mama had to listen to constant demands. Usually she did as he asked and calmed him when his voice got rough. Omakayas didn't understand how Mama could have so much patience sometimes, when her temper was so bad at other times. Yellow Kettle was gentle with Pinch and gentle with Omakayas too. She kept soothing and giving, reassuring them both, and holding Bizheens if he made the slightest sound.

"Your mother has a river of patience," said Nokomis, late the first day, when Omakayas spoke of this. "The river is very broad and deep. But there are big rocks in it!"

It was the first thing that made Omakayas laugh.

"How do you know?" she asked.

"I was like that too. The Anishinabeg study of patience is a lifetime task. You must start young."

"I can't stand Pinch," Omakayas admitted. "He whines, he burns off the feet of my dolls, he tried to steal my red stone. I had to pry it out of his mouth. That's where he was hiding it."

"You love him anyway," said Nokomis.

Omakayas thought of the times Pinch had been her

212

only friend, the times he'd admitted he was scared. She thought of how she'd helped calm him after he cut himself with a hatchet, and remembered the times he'd quietly snuggled close to her when Nokomis told her aadizookaanag. She thought of the time he told her of Two Strike's war. She nodded at Nokomis and then sighed when she looked over at Pinch. He was making a fish trap out of ridiculously long sticks, and using messy ties to fasten the sides and top. His fish trap looked like a goose nest. Omakayas was annoyed with him all over.

"Just look what he's doing!" she said to her grandmother.

Nokomis just shook her head and laughed.

They all had fat and juicy fish that night, for the odd fish trap that Pinch made worked perfectly, of course. Omakayas certainly couldn't complain. There were enough fish to dry in the morning, and extra fish to salt down and sell to the trader. Tomorrow the fish trap would catch more fish to cook for the men when they returned. For although her night was black and deep, her sleep like falling off a cliff, Omakayas had to hope that her dream was true. She hoped, but she really did not know if she should believe.

Why should the spirits tell her things? She was small, she told herself, and ordinary to everybody except Nokomis and Bizheens, and sometimes Old Tallow.

The hours dragged, each longer than the next, and Omakayas grew fearful. Inside, her heart shook. At first she worried that only Miskobines and Little Thunder would return, without Deydey and the priest. Then as her thoughts tried to light here, or there, the concern included Little Thunder. She was startled to realize she worried about him too. Suddenly she felt her heart pinch. She felt sorry for Angeline. How hard it must be for her to miss her beloved Fishtail.

The long afternoon, spent cleaning and skinning fish, dragged to a long shadowed close, and the women went down to the dock to wait for nightfall.

"It means nothing," said Yellow Kettle, "if they don't arrive tonight. It means only that they decided to camp a bit longer. We can't expect them to have Deydey, either. The dream was strong, but there are many ways to see it. The men may be wandering the mainland. So many places they could be . . ."

As Yellow Kettle spoke, Omakayas knew that she was trying desperately to hide her anxiety and to extinguish any hope from forming in her heart. If she had no hope, she would not be disappointed. She could still keep imagining that Deydey was somewhere else, safe, with the hard-traveling priest.

"That soul stealer probably convinced my husband to take him even farther along! Deydey shouldn't listen to him!" As they approached the shore around the dock,

Yellow Kettle's voice became more agitated. Nokomis tried to take Bizheens from her, but Yellow Kettle held on to the baby anxiously, finding comfort in his warmth. Angeline was silent, her look sorrowful and intense. She sat down, in the last of the sun, and stared bleakly out into the ice and waves.

Usually the late sunlight, slanting long beneath the clouds, was Omakayas's favorite time of day. Nokomis had called it the time when the Creator shows us the most beauty in the light, just so that we can remember it in our dreams, and believe in it until the next morning. Omakayas put her hand into her grandmother's hand. Nokomis's hand was tough and kind, just like her. Her touch was gentle, but the strength in her fingers could pull a tough medicine root or pinch off a bleeding vein. Nokomis held Omakayas close, as though one set of thoughts traveled between them. They sat still. They waited. Nobody returned.

That night, everyone slept restlessly. Even Nokomis finally gave up on sleep. Early, while the light was still gray, she was up to boil a tea of medicine barks for Yellow Kettle to drink. Nokomis wanted to strengthen her daughter's blood, for she feared that the worry over Mikwam was beginning to make her skinny. Nokomis filled a makuk with clear, cold water, shaved bark into it, and added some dried leaves of wild raspberry. She heated up a pile of small stones in the fire. Omakayas heard her

215

outside and joined her beside the fire. Together, they used two long ironwood sticks as pincers to remove the red-hot stones. Omakayas dropped each stone into the makuk of water. It sizzled, then sank to the bottom, heating the water. The tea was ready for Yellow Kettle when she dragged herself from the cabin. Gratefully, she sipped it. Suddenly, her face brightened.

"You know how things happen when you don't expect them?" she asked, "Let's not expect anything today!"

That day was better then because instead of waiting they made themselves very, very busy. Nokomis set up the hide stretcher and Omakayas went to work scraping a deerskin. Angeline finished Fishtail's vest, and hung it out for everyone to admire. Pinch made yet another fish trap, stranger than the other. This one looked like a crazed beaver had got hold of it and chewed on it. He was very proud of his work and went down to set it in the water. Two Strike came by, jumping into the camp with a great shout, and they sent her down to put the fish trap in with Pinch. Twilight, Little Bee, and Auntie Muskrat came over to stay with them. They made a great pot of soup. They gathered and cut wood. Nokomis carefully examined the canoe and painted its seams with her special caulking mixture of pinesap and charcoal. Yellow Kettle growled under her breath, breathing fire at the priest, swearing he was the cause of this and many other miseries they faced ever since the first black robe appeared in their land.

"We should send them back to where the sun comes up," she said in a menacing voice. She stopped work to sit near Omakayas and rest. "You have done well with your dog," she noticed, after a time. Makataywazi sat alertly next to Omakayas as she worked, and often attended to the others, but liked being close to his favorite human.

"Meegwech," said Omakayas. Any praise from her mother was rare and, given the way she felt about dogs, this was a special tribute.

Auntie Muskrat had some lead and decided to use Deydey's bullet mold to make some bullets. Everyone was concentrating on some task when Makataywazi whined, jumped up, and sped into the woods. Only Omakayas noticed and, before she could drop everything and follow, the lost ones returned. Deydey, Miskobines, Old Tallow, and Little Thunder were suddenly in the camp. Omakayas caught sight of Deydey first, but he put a finger to his lips and indicated that she be quiet. Yellow Kettle had her back to him. With one foot, she was jiggling Bizheens in his cradle board. In her lap, there was a great mound of diaper cattail fluff that she was cleaning and stuffing into a woven string bag. Silently, Deydey crept up to her. He plucked a thin twig, kneeled behind her, and lightly touched her neck. Yellow Kettle slapped her neck. He touched the side of her ear. She grabbed at air. He touched the top of her head.

"Gego, Pinch!" said Yellow Kettle.

Deydey almost laughed. He touched the side of her cheek.

"Pinch!" Mama jumped up in a sudden rage and fell into her husband's arms. Emotions clashed in her face—irritation turned to shock. Wonder overcame her, and then simple joy. Mama buried her face in Deydey's shirt and her shoulders shook in a combination of tears and laughter.

The feast they had was not only to celebrate the return of the men, but to honor a powerful dreamer. That is what the gray and wise Miskobines called Omakayas when he heard the story of what she'd done. Omakayas herself felt as though she were in a dream. She really hadn't tried to dream, or asked for a dream, or done anything but put out tobacco for the spirits. And yet this dream had chosen her. The dream had saved her father. For he and Father Baraga were indeed on that island of the eagles and they were stranded. At the feast, Deydey told the story of what had happened.

THE ICE CANOE

"When we got to the place of the far point people," said Deydey, "they had moved on except for two families, both of whom were already baptized. Father Baraga was happy enough to deliver their ceremony, and then we started back for home. Partway back, it seemed to me that we shouldn't go as we'd come. I told the priest we must go the long way around. We must go where there was no current under the ice. I feared there would be a breakup soon."

Deydey stopped, shook his head at the stubbornness of the Black Robe.

"I told him that the air smelled like the ice would break. Baraga said no. He insisted we go the way we came. The priest and I sat down and argued. I gave him every reason not to go that way. Still, he insisted. Feeling heavy-hearted then, I followed. Not fifty paces out, the ice went. It cracked all around us in big chunks. The whole lake ripped up. If I wasn't so afraid, myself, I would have laughed at Father Baraga's face!

"'We are going back,' I said, and now Baraga followed me. But we were too late! At the end of the ice we saw a widening river of water. We were on a narrow piece of ice. As we stood there we saw the swift, black water, deadly cold, gnashing between us and the safe ground. Then our ice started to move! So there we were, on an ice canoe, traveling the lake. We all know and have seen these pieces of ice—they drift for a moon in the lakes, shrinking, until they go back into the water. I thought of swimming for shore, but I knew the cold of the water would kill me before I got there. We were heading for the open."

Everyone was silent. Even Old Tallow's breath came quickly, and she leaned forward to hear better.

"All that day, we drifted wide, according to the wind. But I could feel the wind changing and I had my blanket with me, luckily. I stretched it out for a sail and steered us by standing this way to the wind, that way to the wind."

Deydey jumped up and demonstrated his desperate stretching, and everyone laughed.

"By afternoon," he went on, "I thought we had a chance. Father Baraga had sank onto his knees and I couldn't rouse him; he was praying to his good spirit. At the same time, I had put my tobacco in the water, praying to every spirit who had helped me in the past. I stayed in place with my blanket, gathering wind. Just before dusk, I managed to steer our ice close to an island. I coaxed the wind to come behind us and push us to the shore of that island. And it did. We stepped off the ice as though we were delivered there from a real canoe. Baraga staggered up the bank and kissed the ground, our mother, and then he said to me that his God had answered his prayers.

"'It was *my* spirits who answered *my* prayers,' I informed him. 'And the sail I made out of my blanket!'

"'Oh no,' said Father Baraga, 'that cannot be.'

"'My spirits live around here,' I told him.

"'Mine is the real one, and the most powerful.'

"And so, ridiculously, we argued in our relief and gratitude. The argument kept on the next day, and even into the next. Perhaps we needed to argue in order not to dwell on the fact that there were only two ways to get off the island. One was death. The other was rescue by a passing boat. As we were in a most remote place, the first was most likely. I hated to tell him, but after we had divided up our tiny store of food and eaten it, I began to prepare my mind for death."

There was a deep silence in the lodge. It was Miskobines who spoke, this time directly to Omakayas. His kind eyes held hers as he spoke.

"You have done a great thing in saving your father's life, and the life of this priest who loves us—or at least loves to collect our spirits! Gizhe Manidoo gave you a very great gift, but you must remember that this gift does not belong to you. This gift is for the good of your people. Use it to help them, never to gain power for yourself. For as soon as you misuse this gift, it will leave you. Mi'iw minik!"

Miskobines had spoken very wisely, and Omakayas would always remember his words. Even as he said them, it was as though he was reading her mind. For she was thinking how much better the thing she had done was than Two Strike's moose. Two Strike had made a lucky shot, but Omakayas had actually had a dream that saved the life of her own father. Omakayas was wondering just how she would act toward Two Strike now, and whether she would accept if Two Strike asked her to join her war party. She couldn't turn around and look at Two Strike, but she was picturing the sour envy on her cousin's face, and then Miskobines spoke. Omakayas sighed and looked down at her feet. Anyway, to her great surprise, when she did sneak a look at Two Strike, her cousin looked at her not with envy but with admiration.

Two Strike's unexpected goodwill shamed Omakayas. After all of the bad thoughts she had had about Two Strike, her cousin's rageful heart was gallant and free of jealousy. Omakayas felt humbled. She was nothing, it was true. She was insignificant and small. But then she looked at Deydey and he looked back at her. There was a warm and shining light in his eyes. Warmer, brighter, it told her she was not ordinary. Not to him. Not at all.

That night, Omakayas was sleeping very deeply and at first, when Angeline whispered in her ear, the sound became a part of her dream.

"Dream for me, sister," said Angeline, "dream of Fishtail. Tell me where he is. Tell me if he lives. Tell me that Fishtail is all right."

Omakayas heard her, then slipped back into her sleep. She asked for a dream, but no special knowledge came. The next morning, there was nothing to say. If only she could dream when she wanted to, not only when the spirits chose to send her messages. Perhaps she did have to go out, take the charcoal, fast for knowledge. If only she was in control of this strange gift she was given, a gift she couldn't count on or predict.

FIFTEEN

ALONE WITH THE SPIRITS

One morning Omakayas woke up to find Nokomis sitting beside her. She smiled, snuggled deeper into her blanket, and was about to doze off again when Nokomis touched her face. Omakayas opened her eyes. In her hand, Nokomis held a lump of charcoal. Omakayas's chest pinched. If she took the charcoal, she would be sent out to the woods to fast and to listen for her spirits. She closed her eyes. She didn't want to go. She didn't want to! A thread of fear shot, icy cold, up the middle of her stomach.

"Oh please, Nokomis," she whispered, squeezing her eyes tightly shut and turning away.

"You will never control this gift," said Nokomis. "All you can do is try to understand why it is given to you."

"How do I do that?" mumbled Omakayas, burrowing deeper into her blanket.

Nokomis shook her head and smiled without speaking, as if to say that Omakayas herself knew the answer.

"I will help you," said Nokomis, "we will do this in a special way."

Omakayas stayed very still, breathing hard a long while, before she finally turned back to Nokomis, took the charcoal from her hand, and slowly rubbed it across her face.

That morning, Nokomis went off into the woods for a long time. When she returned, she took Omakayas's hand and said to Mama and Deydey, "Your daughter is ready."

Yellow Kettle stood up and opened her arms. She put her arms around Omakayas and for a moment Omakayas closed her eyes and wished, deeply, with all of her heart, that she could be little again, like Bizheens. She wanted to roll up in a fur bag and sleep in her mother's arms. But her eyes opened and Deydey was before her now. In his hands, he held his sacred pipe, which he carried in a buckskin bag that Mama had beaded for him with beautiful flowers.

"Take this with you, keep it close," he said.

Omakayas was so overwhelmed that she couldn't speak. Deydey regarded his pipe as a living being, as his grandfather. Omakayas was almost afraid to hold the pipe, but when she did cradle it against her, she somehow felt better. Deydey smoothed his hands over her hair and he kissed the part in her hair. He told her that he would be near, that he would check on Omakayas several times a day, but she wouldn't see him. Nokomis would camp nearby, too. They would not let anything happen to her. Omakayas appreciated everything that her father said, but she couldn't tell him that he and everyone else misunderstood her fear. She was not afraid of animals, not afraid of snakes, creeping things, or any kind of weather. She was not afraid of the dark and not even afraid of owls. She was not afraid of the cold and, besides, she would have a fire. Hunger did not scare her. She had survived hunger. No, what they didn't understand and what she couldn't say was what she'd said to Pinch. She was afraid of her dreams. She both wanted to know, and didn't want to know, what they might tell her. Their power frightened her. They were so real, so shattering, full of such joy and sorrow. Sometimes they were just too much to feel.

As Omakayas followed Nokomis into the woods a bush beside her wobbled strangely.

"Sss!" It was Pinch. He thrust his hand from the leaves. He had stolen strips of jerky from mother's drying rack and something else wrapped in bark. "Sister, take these!" he whispered. Omakayas took the jerky although she knew she wouldn't eat it. She opened the birchbark package and found an awkwardly constructed sabeys, or dream catcher. Pinch had done what he could to take care of her. Omakayas's throat burned, her eyes hurt with tears. He wasn't an awful brother, not really. In fact, he sometimes understood her best of anyone in the world.

"You'll camp here," said Nokomis, indicating a soft place in a pine bough shelter just below a huge tree. The trunk of the pine was as big around as a wigwam. Low, comfortable branches led upward like steps. It was such a homey place to make a camp that for the first time Omakayas felt some of her anxious fear lessen.

"I'll be close," said Nokomis. "I'll bring a little water to you every day and I'll smoke my pipe and pray." She carried a bag that contained the rabbit-skin blanket she had made for Omakayas, and when she shook it out and placed it in the corner of the little pine bough shelter, Omakayas could almost imagine that she'd be all right, that she'd be comfortable, that nothing frightening or out of the ordinary would happen to her. As Nokomis disappeared into the undergrowth to make her own camp, Omakayas thought how most who went looking for a vision were probably hoping for an extraordinary spirit, a lightning bolt expression, an amazing protector to befriend them. Omakayas wanted the opposite. As she placed Pinch's dream catcher over the entrance to her little shelter, she prayed for nothing to happen.

The first day, and also the second, she got her wish.

The hours passed in a dreamy fog. Omakayas was not to leave the spot Nokomis had chosen, and she sat quietly holding her father's pipe or lay cuddled in her rabbit blanket and stared up into the boughs of the pines. When she could bear her thirst no longer she sipped from the bag of water that Nokomis had left with her. After the first day her hunger dulled to a low ache. She knew she'd have hunger pains in another day, but for a while it was not so bad. Her mind felt very clear. Every so often she wished she had something to do with her hands, but she wasn't supposed to distract herself that way. Instead, Nokomis had taught her to sing several songs. One song was about the four directions—east, south, west, north. She sang to each of the directions at sunrise and sunset. Another song was a request for protection from the spirits. She was careful never to sing that one too loudly, in case some extra-powerful spirit whose attention she didn't want to attract might hear. The song that Omakayas liked best was one that Nokomis had composed to that her guiding spirit, the memegwesi. If she had to see a spirit, Omakayas thought she wouldn't mind seeing the funny little man whom her grandmother had described. But nothing happened. To Omakayas's great relief the hours passed, not unpleasantly, in listening to the sounds of the woods and watching the slow progress of shadows and light.

On the third day, things got more difficult. Suddenly, Omakayas became so ragingly hungry that she put a couple of pine needles into her mouth to chew. Her stomach hurt constantly now. She was dizzy when she stood up too fast. Her legs wobbled. Tears came into her eyes and welled out and coursed down her cheeks as she thought in turn of everybody in her family and wished she could be with them. Finally, Omakayas could not stand it anymore. Nokomis had told her that if things got to be too much or she was ever afraid she should tie Deydey's pipe onto her back and climb the tree. Omakayas did exactly this, and although she was worried that she might get dizzy she was fine. She felt better and better as she progressed from limb to limb. Where the limbs formed a nest, she sat looking down at the world. She hadn't been there long at all when she heard twigs snapping. There was a bearish grunting, a shivering croon that mother bears make, just below her tree.

There they were, at the base—a heavy mother bear shedding patches of fur and her little winter-born cub. The mother reared up on her hind legs and stretched her neck, nose working, as she tried to figure out with her weak eyes who perched above her.

"So, you've come to see me," said Omakayas.

Although she respected bears and stayed out of their way, she was not afraid of them. She was in fact comforted by their presence now. The mother showed no signs of wanting to climb her tree. They were only curious. And after all, it was the bear people who had taught Nokomis medicine. Nokomis had often shown Omakayas signs of where bears dug rocks or tore leaves, roots, and fruit into their mouths. She said that bears used plants to heal themselves just like humans. It was important to watch them very closely to see what plants they ate and which they avoided. The mother sniffed around Omakayas's camp, no doubt hoping she'd find a scrap or two to eat, while her baby played by swinging himself up limb by limb toward Omakayas. He was so young he still had some of his downy baby fuzz. He climbed until he reached a branch just level with Omakayas. From there, he watched her with wide, intent, serious eyes. He seemed to be wondering just how he should treat this new animal. Was she another cub of some kind? Would she play with him? Why did she make such peculiar sounds?

"Hello, little brother," she kindly said.

The cub's mouth opened in fascination when Omakayas talked to him. She asked him all of the usual questions one might ask of any new acquaintance—what he liked to do best of all, and what to eat, whether he had brothers and sisters and whether his mother minded if he stared at girl beings. The little bear said nothing. His eyes did not move. They stayed fixed on Omakayas with the utmost gravity. When Omakayas fell silent, he continued to look at her. He held her gaze for such a long time that she almost imagined he was going to say something himself. But he only climbed down the tree, after a while. As soon as he reached the bottom of the tree, he and his mother disappeared into the woods as quickly as they'd come. Omakayas stayed sitting in the tree. There was something about the way they had visited her so politely, and lingered in her presence, then left with a subdued quietness, that reminded Omakayas of the way people visit when they've come to say good-bye.

Long after the bears had left, Omakayas sat in the tree watching the world around her. She stayed there until the sun lowered and the air suddenly chilled. Climbing down, her arms shook and her legs were stiff and weak. She had to be very careful not to fall. At the base of the tree, she crawled into her shelter. She rolled up in her blanket and decided to go to sleep without making a fire. *The time is almost up*, she thought, *and nothing has happened! Even* before her thought ended, sleep took her, and she washed beneath consciousness swift as a leaf.

Omakayas felt herself drifting along between sleeping and waking. She let herself go. It was then that she found herself walking toward the beach with her arms full of bundles. She understood that the bears had said good-bye to her because she was going away. Then Omakayas and her family were crammed with all of their possessions into their canoes. They traveled swiftly, skimming over water, down rivers, always together in temporary camps at night. They came to a beautiful lake filled with hundreds of islands, only Omakayas saw them as spirits. Those spirits welcomed them. The family lived in this lake full of spirits. She saw her little brothers grow. Her mother and father looked at her. Their hair was white. And yet again she saw herself, traveling by land this time. A tall man walked beside her. She could not see his face. The world around them was vast, flat, endless, and eternal as the great lake around her island. The sky was huge with mountainous formations of clouds and she could see from one end of it to the other, in every direction. The grass flowed like water from where she stood and she felt herself continuing on. There was a cabin, not of cedar, but some other kind of log. A team of horses and a long birchbark bundle. Terrible sorrow passed through her but then there were children before her eyes, ten children chasing one another, plump and bold and laughing. Some looked like

Pinch, some like Bizheens. Some looked like Omakayas herself. They ran into the cabin and came out with an old woman, a white-haired smiling woman. They held her arms and guided her along to a chair set underneath a leafy arbor. Omakayas realized that the old woman was blind, though she had a strong step, and that the children were guiding her direction. Some of the children stayed with her and some ran away. She began to talk to the children. She was telling them stories. Her hands moved, making pictures in the air. The old woman made a cawing sound and her hands flapped like a bird's. Omakayas understood that the old woman was herself, telling about the crow Andeg she'd had as a young girl. Omakayas floated deeper, into a lightless place. Scenes appeared, events in this woman's life—some small and some big, wrenching, full of great joy. The events occurred so quickly that she couldn't remember them all, though she'd try time and time again, over the coming year, for the vision she received and the stories she told, the scenes of emotion, good and bad, that she endured, was the story of her life. She had been shown the shape of it.

When Nokomis came to get her, Omakayas was sitting beneath the tree with Deydey's pipe cradled in her arms. Nokomis sat down before her.

"What did you see?" she asked.

"Everything," Omakayas answered.

SIXTEEN

THE RETURN
AND THE DEPARTURE

When Fishtail returned on the edge of nightfall, the water was so slick and so still that the colors of the sunset pooled, lazily motionless. He dug his paddle in the red reflection of the sun, again and again, until finally the last stroke that drove him to the island. Children playing on the dock saw him and shouted. One ran to tell the grown-ups and soon everyone was at the shore, eager but anxious. Angeline ran so swiftly that no one could catch her. Only her happiness at Fishtail's return was uncomplicated. For others, there would be bad news.

Omakayas ran behind her, and then stood frozen on the shore outside the crowd clustered in front of Fishtail and her sister. She could see Angeline. She was almost alarmed, for it seemed to Omakayas that the last of the sun had entered her sister's face. Angeline glowed with a hazardous-looking warmth. Her cheeks were flaming red and her eyes glittered as though with a fever. In fact, if Omakayas didn't know that Angeline had been just fine, having been helping her haul in fishing nets just before Fishtail arrived, she would have thought that her sister was really ill.

Fishtail was the same. Though gaunt and weary, he was so glad to see Angeline that the two rushed together with no notice of anyone else. They hugged so hard and for so long that the little boys started making kissing noises, laughing at them. They broke apart and grinned at each other in amazement.

When Fishtail saw Omakayas, his face lighted up and he bent and scooped her into his arms. He squeezed her so tight that she couldn't breathe. Tears started into her eyes, but she blinked them back only to have them burn and fall, later that night, when he spoke.

For although Fishtail had returned, he spoke of the others who had died of the rotten pork and spoiled provisions. By the time he finished his report, there was only silence and weeping in the lodge. Fishtail said that he knew it would take the Ojibwe a very long time to recover from the loss. But still the government had not retreated from its position. The Ojibwe were being forced west, into the country of the Bwaanag, away from their gardens, away from their ancestors' graves, away from their fishing grounds, away from their lodges and cabins and all that made the island home.

After Fishtail delivered his message, there was a profound silence. He said that that the agent of the United States government would arrive in only days to make the official announcement. Omakayas slipped away and hardly knew where she was walking. It was not until she found herself sitting on her favorite rock, one that jutted far out into the water. It was not until she was surrounded by water and lulled by waves, that she dared to feel the other waves that stormed through her heart. In the great dream of her life, which she had seen when she was alone in the woods, all that would happen had appeared before her. She had seen the message, though not the messenger. She had seen the shock of sorrow and the gathering of strength. She had seen the going away. Now it was happening. She was experiencing in truth what she dreaded, what she had seen. Omakayas looked around her at the still beach and listened to the ever talking waves. *All things change, all things change*, they said to her. *All things change, even us, even you.*

Omakayas closed her eyes and strained her hearing. She listened until her heart burned, but the waves said nothing else to her, so she left the rock and walked to the place where her little brother Neewo was buried. In her pocket, she had a piece of precious maple sugar. When she came to the small rectangular house that was built on top of the grave, Omakayas put the sugar lump on the sill of the tiny window that Deydey had built into the western end.

"Here, take this, little brother," said Omakayas. Then she sat in the long grass and let the sobs out, the tears flow down, let all of the sadness break out of her. "I don't know where we are going," she told Neewo. "But your spirit must watch out for us. Help us from your world."

There was no answer, only silence, a light breeze in the grass. The moon, when it rose shedding its kind light, had nothing to say to her either. Only when Omakayas let her mind grow very calm could she read what her heart was telling her to do. You will not take leave of your beloved and beautiful home in bitterness or in anger. You will not take leave in hatred. You are stronger than that. When the Anishinabeg must give way to a stronger force, they do so with the dignity of love. You will leave your home in gratitude for what the Gizhe Manidoo, the great and kind spirit, has given to you. All the spirits will help you, even the tiniest, your brother. Your heart is good. You are blessed. Go forward into your life.

Nokomis sat on a woven pukwe mat, her bundles spread all around her—bark-wrapped packets, sweet grass twined together in braids, roots sewed into rings or wound into balls and tied. She had a little bag of crushed, dried honey-bees. There was a small birchbark box that contained the puffball dust that Omakayas had helped her collect. Nokomis undid the string bags that held her seeds, and Omakayas helped her to pack them tightly into smaller containers.

There were corn kernels, tiny and pointed, bright red. She had traded with an Odaawa woman long ago for that special corn. The kernels puffed when heated in the fire and made a delicious treat. There were pale yellow kernels of corn and speckled blue kernels. Omakayas helped Nokomis pack the mottled beans, the squash and pump-kin seeds, the dried-out bits of the blue potatoes they loved to dig and roast. At last, all of the seeds were neatly fit together in a large makuk with a birchbark top that Nokomis tied down. The two looked at the square box. Omakayas lifted it. The box was heavy.

"Not all that heavy when you think there's a whole garden inside of it."

"Not all that heavy," agreed Nokomis. Her eyes were sad, but she was proud of what she saved.

"Nokomis?" Omakayas was almost afraid to ask something that had bothered her ever since she knew that they must leave. Nokomis looked at her quietly, waiting for the question.

Omakayas tried to find the words, for it was a personal question, and she wanted to ask as carefully as possible. She was afraid to make Nokomis sadder than she already was.

"You know you can ask me anything," said Nokomis. "Don't be afraid."

"Well, Nookoo, I was just wondering about your little memegwesi, your helper. Can he follow us? Will he know where you are?"

Nokomis looked at her in surprise, then she smiled.

"How good you are to think of your grandmother, when you are so troubled yourself." She put her arm around Omakayas's shoulder, and indeed, her voice was very sad when she spoke.

"I have left tobacco where I think my little friend will find it, and some cloth, too, for a special set of clothes. It does break my heart to leave the place where he found me, and helped me, so long ago. But my granddaughter, the memegwesiwag have relatives all through this land. Perhaps he will send word to his cousins across the bay, perhaps he will ask them to care for these persons who must leave their home, perhaps they will be waiting for us, watching over us. That's what I hope."

Omakayas put her arms around her grandma and held her tightly. It was the best thing she'd heard all day. With a calmer heart, she went back to the cabin with Nokomis and helped her decide what to pack.

❋   ❋   ❋

All that they possessed and had collected over the years on the island was before them. There were the special hoes—the moose horn, the iron, the one of an antler that Omakayas used. These they had to leave. Omakayas's gun barrel scraper was too heavy to take along, and even though Deydey had given it to her, she left it without a great sense of loss. Too many times she'd used it to scrape those stinking hides! Her rabbit-skin blanket was rolled and stuffed into a pack that she would carry on the difficult portages. Of course, she took her doll, the one Deydey had made for her, and its cradle board. She put it carefully into a skin back that she would wear on her shoulder. Her winter dress and the beautiful shawl that Angeline had made for her came too. She took her mittens and her winter makazinan. She made a rack of their snowshoes. They took makuks of maple sugar, dried fish, what remained of last year's rice. In the end, they left a great deal behind with the few families whose people were too old to travel, or sick, or who preferred to try their luck and remain behind.

They could not take their cabin, their sweet cedar cabin by the pine, and they could not take Makataywazi.

"There's just no room for the dog," said Yellow Kettle, and she spoke as gently as she could, for she knew how Omakayas felt about her dog. "If we take the dog, we'll have to leave one of us behind. We don't have enough room and besides, we are going into dangerous country. We can't have barking dogs."

"I bet Old Tallow will not leave her dogs behind," Omakayas said in a tiny, stubborn voice.

"Her dogs are older, perfectly trained," said Yellow Kettle. "Her dogs are all that she has."

Omakayas sat for a long time with Makataywazi, down on the shore, on the rock where she'd said her good-bye. Together, they watched the unchanging line of dark green across the bay. Not only would her dog stay here, but her crow, Andeg, had not come back yet. He would find them gone when he returned from his winter hunting grounds. Omakayas forgot all of the strength she gained, the gratitude, and she wanted to sob with fury. She tried a few deep sighs, even tried to make crying sounds, but her sadness and anger was too big. It was a stone. A smooth stone with no chips or cracks.

"Ombay," she said to her dog, and Makataywazi jumped up in such a concerned way that Omakayas knew he understood. The dog wagged his tail and grinned as though to say he'd be all right, and so would Omakayas, and not to worry. Things could be worse. But Omakayas already knew what she would do, and the thought made her more cheerful. She would roll Makataywazi into her rabbit-skin blanket and hide her dog in the canoe. By the time anybody knew she had taken her dog along, it would be too late. They would be far out on the water.

ANGELINE AND FISHTAIL

When everything was packed down to the shore, and loaded into the canoes, Omakayas noticed that Angeline was loading her things in the canoe that Fishtail came home in, and she was glad. The night before, they had gone somewhere together and that morning they'd talked to Deydey, Yellow Kettle, and Nokomis.

Now, with everyone assembled and ready to leave, there was a pause. Everyone stopped what they were doing and sat down. Miskobines, Deydey, and Fishtail took out their pipes and sat together. The women sat with them while the men smoked and prayed. Then Nokomis brought out a beautiful piece of red cloth and tied Angeline's hand to Fishtail's hand. The two sat together. Fishtail wore the beautiful beaded vest that Angeline had made for him. The vines twisted up each side of his chest and the flowers gleamed in the morning light. His face was starved and thin, but he was handsome with his carved cheeks and thick hair down to his shoulders.

"Children," said Miskobines, "you have decided to spend your life with one another. You have decided that you love each other and want to walk the same road. This is the beginning. From here, we don't know where we go.

Only proceed along this path with love, and you will find the strength."

He put his arms around them both and embraced them. Then Old Tallow came up to the two. She stood before them, scowling, and it was clear that she wanted to speak. Several times she opened her mouth, but every time she did, the wrong words seemed to jump from her lips.

"I was married twice, no, three times . . . I scared away my husbands, but . . . no. You are married, but you have no dogs . . . no." Finally she gave up, threw her head forward in a belligerent way, and then growled at Fishtail. "You be good to her or else!" She thrust a beautifully tanned lynx skin at them and stomped off to see to her own canoe. In turn, everybody went up to Fishtail and Angeline, held their hands, wished blessings upon them, or just hugged them tight.

Then it really was time to go. Around them, a few curious chimookoman people stood watching. One of them was the Break-Apart Girl. She came to Omakayas and in her hand she had a piece of cloth stitched carefully with letters. The Break-Apart Girl pointed at the letters, then at Omakayas, then at herself, and spoke the same words over and over.

"I can't tell what she is saying," Omakayas finally said to Deydey, who spoke the trader's English. Although he frowned to be taken from his task, for he was busy, he stepped near and looked down at the piece of cloth. The two of them worked out the meaning of the letters.

"I think this is your name, how she hears it." Deydey pointed at some of the tracks. "And this is her name. She made this cloth for you and wanted to give it to you. She wants you to remember her."

Omakayas flung her arms around the Break-Apart Girl and hugged her, feeling as though her stone heart would crack. She was surprised that the girl cared for her, and the gift made her happy in spite of the tremendous sorrow of leaving.

"I'll keep it always," she said. The little tan dots on the Break-Apart Girl's face went a rosy red and she smiled. Yellow Kettle gave Bizheens to Omakayas to hold while she prepared the canoe, and the girls tickled him and cooed at him. Omakayas wished the moment wouldn't end and yet at the same time she was aware of the time pressing down.

Suddenly, there was a commotion in the canoe that Omakayas had packed, and she turned in time to see that the rabbit blanket, bundled carefully around Makataywazi, had flung itself out of the canoe and was bouncing around on the ground and it was barking and growling. One of the village dogs had come too close, and Makataywazi had not been able to contain himself. He was trying to protect her family, even though he was tied up in the blanket!

Omakayas ran for her dog, still carrying Bizheens. When he saw the bundle bouncing comically up and down along the shore, he threw his arms out. His little mouth opened wide, and he made a rusty little sound. The sound got bigger, more definite. Bizheens seemed to concentrate. His whole face crinkled into a laughing expression, and then the actual laugh came out. A big laugh. A baby's belly laugh. His very first laugh! It was a laugh that would have made Omakayas laugh too, except that her dog was going to be discovered.

Quick as a flash, Yellow Kettle untied the blanket and Makataywazi sprang free and bounded proudly to Omakayas. Bizheens was still laughing, delighted. Omakayas wanted to take heart from this good moment, which happened in the midst of sadness, but at the same time she knew she would be parted from Makataywazi. Shaking her head, Yellow Kettle called to Omakayas.

"You know he can't come along with us."

There was no choice. Omakayas put Bizheens down and knelt with her sweet dog, her cheerful and generous companion. The Break-Apart Girl patted Makataywazi too, and although it hurt her heart, Omakayas knew that there was nothing else that she could do. She pointed to the dog, and then to her friend. To her friend, the Break-Apart Girl, and then to the dog. She brought her hands together. Omakayas rubbed her face in Makataywazi's rough fur, and then she gently took the Break-Apart Girl's hand and put it on her dog.

"Keep him, be good to him," she said in a choked voice.

The Break-Apart Girl nodded. She understood. She nodded and petted Makataywazi as Omakayas left, again holding Bizheens. As they got into the canoe, she heard Makataywazi bark, but she did not turn around. She could not turn around. She tried to remember what the waves told her. What her dream showed. She tried to remember how all things change and to go with gratitude. But she wanted to cry, or shout. Her throat burned. Her eyes stung. A great roar built around her and she was afraid to look at all that she was leaving behind.

OLD TALLOW'S JEEMAAN

Now it was clear. Old Tallow had made the odd canoe, with the little roof to tie down, so that she would have a place for her dogs to travel when they all left together. Her cabin, stuffed with kettles, knives, skins, rags, bolts of fabric, brass pails, and assorted junk, could hardly be emptied into one canoe. She sold what she could to the trader and gave the rest away. Old Tallow stuffed as much as she could into her canoe, and then called her dogs. They came, each bounding into his or her place, some nestling in their little house in the rear of the jeemaan. Those that stayed out sat in the canoe with such authority that they looked as though they should be paddling too.

As the little party made its way across the water, the dogs silently watched the waves and seemed to wisely anticipate their progress. They were not worried. They knew that wherever they were going Old Tallow would take care of them. They had no fear.

Sitting in the center of her family's canoe with Bizheens, Omakayas decided that she would be like the dogs. The breeze was stiff, and Deydey and Yellow Kettle bent to their paddles with strong pulls. It is hard to stay unhappy out on

246

the water, in a canoe. Even the sorrow of leaving the island was soothed a little by the smell of water, the glitter of the waves, the cries of the gulls, the sight of one lone circling eagle who watched over them from above.

Omakayas's heart lifted, in spite of herself, as they neared the great rose-red beaches of the opposite shore and began to paddle along the edge of the lake. They paddled onward. They sang together, traveling songs that helped keep their paddling coordinated and helped their spirits rise. Deydey's deep voice rose high and then Fishtail joined him from the next canoe. Even Pinch, who rode with Fishtail, Angeline, and Nokomis, sang those traveling songs. The women joined in, at a higher pitch, and once Old Tallow's dogs even tried to howl before she shut them up with a sharp command.

Everything changed when they entered the mouth of the river.

Omakayas could feel the difference as they left the bright, open spaces of the island and the big lake, and went into the mouth of the mainland stream. Soon the leaves closed overhead. The air went dappled green. The river was a narrow road of water through the tree-confined woods of the country of the dangerous Bwaanag. The little family drew their canoes close together. Nokomis sang, in a very low voice, the song that introduced the game of silence. But this time there were no prizes. This time there would be no laughter if some child mistakenly spoke. The game was very different now and everyone knew it. Along the shore there were ears, and eyes, and enemies who resented the Ojibwe entering their territory and would gladly attack. Fishtail and Deydey kept lookout. They traveled swiftly, and without rest. The children bit their lips and held their tongues, for they all understood, even Pinch, that the game of silence was now a game of life and death.

Yet through the flickering new leaves, with the shadows that raced across the water, among the bars and rods of sunlight that rode up and down the tree trunks, Omakayas thought she saw other spirits, good ones, perhaps the relatives of Nokomis's little helper, and she threw her heart out before them. She gazed into the crush of green. Here, after all, was not only danger but possibility. Here was adventure. Here was the next life they would live together on this earth.

AUTHOR'S NOTE
ON THE OJIBWE LANGUAGE

Obijwemowin was originally a spoken, not written, language, and for that reason spellings are often idiosyncratic. There are also many, many dialects in use. To make the Obijwemowin in the text easier to read, I have often used phonetic spellings. I apologize to the reader for any mistakes and refer those who would like to encounter the language in depth to *A Concise Dictionary of Minnesota Ojibwe*, edited by John D. Nichols and Earl Nyholm; to the *Oshkaabewis Native Journal*, edited by Anton Treurer; and to the curriculum developed by Dennis Jones at the University of Minnesota.

GLOSSARY AND PRONUNCIATION
GUIDE OF OJIBWE TERMS

aadizookaan (ahd-zoh-kahn): a traditional story that often helps explain how to live as an Ojibwe

aadizookaanag (ahd-zoh-kahn-ahg): the plural form of aadizookaan

abwi (ab-wih): paddle

ahneen (ah-NEEN): a greeting, sometimes in the form of a question

akik (ah-keik): kettle

aneendi g'deydey (ah-NEEN-dih gih-day-day): where is your father?

Anishinabe (AH-nish-in-AH-bay): the original name for the Ojibwe or Chippewa people, a Native American group who originated in and live mainly in the northern North American woodlands. There are currently Ojibwe reservations in Michigan, Wisconsin, Minnesota, North Dakota, Ontario, Manitoba, Montana, and Saskatchewan.

Anishinabeg (AH-nish-in-AH-bayg): the plural form of Anishinabe

asin (ah-sin): stone

asiniig (ah-sin-ig): the plural form of asin

awakaanag (ah-wah-kahn-ahg): domestic animals

ayah (ah-YAH): yes

bawa'iganakoog (bah-wah'ih-gahn-a-koog): rice knockers

biboon (bih-BOON): winter

binesi (bin-AY-sih): thunderbird

binesiwag (bin-AY-sih-wug): the plural form of binesi

booni'aa (BOO-nee-ah): leave it alone

Bwaanag (BWAHN-ug): the Dakota and Lakota people, another Native tribe, whose reservations spread across the Great Plains

chimookoman (chi-MOOK-oh-man): word meaning "big knife," used to describe white people or non-Indians

chimookomanag (chi-MOOK-oh-man-ug): the plural form of chimookoman

daga (dah-gah): please

dagwaging (dah-GWAG-ing): fall

Deydey (DAY-day): Daddy

eya' (ey-ah): yes

ezhichigeyan (ey-zhi-chi-GAY-an): to be doing something

ganabaj (gah-nah-BUTCH): maybe

gaween (gah-WEEN): no

geegoonyag (ghee-goon-yag): fish

geewen (gee-WEH): go home

geget (GEH-geht): surely, or for emphasis, truly or really

geget sa (GEH-geht sah): surely, with more emphasis

gego (GAY-go): exclamation meaning "stop that"

gichi-oodenan (gih-chi-oo-day-nahn): cities

gigawaabamin (gih-gah-WAH-bah-min): I will see you

ginebig (gih-NAY-big): snake

ginebigoog (gih-NAY-big-ook): the plural form of ginebig

gisina (gih-sin-ah): to be cold

gizhawenimin (gih-zha-WAY-nih-min): I love you

Gizhe Manidoo (Gih-zhay Man-ih-do): the great, kind spirit

gookoosh (goo-KOOSH): pig

gookooshag (goo-KOOSH-ug): the plural form of gookoosh

hiyn (high-n): exclamation of sympathy or chagrin, meaning "that's too bad"

howah (HOW-ah): a sound of approval

ishkodewaaboo (ish-KODAY-wah-boo): alcohol

ishtay (ISH-tay): exclamation meaning how good, nice, pleasant

izhadah (iz-yah-dah): let's go

jeemaan (jee-mahn): canoe

jeemaanan (jee-MAHN-an): the plural form of jeemaan

majigoode (mah-ji-GOO-day): dress

makakoon (mah-kah-koon): the plural form of makuk

makazin (MAH-kah-zin): footwear usually made of tanned moose hide or deerskin, often trimmed with beads and/or fur

makazinan (MAH-kah-zin-ahn): plural form of makazin

makuk (mah-KUK): a container of birchbark folded and often stitched together with basswood fiber. Ojibwe people use these containers today, especially for traditional feasts

Manidoo (Mah-nih-do): god, spirit

manoomin (mah-NOH-min): wild rice; the word means "the good seed"

mashkiki (mahsh-kih-kih): medicine

meegwech (mee-gwetch): thank you

memegwesi (may-may-gway-see): little person

memegwesiwag (may-may-gway-see-wug): the plural form of memegwesi

Midewiwin (mih-DAY-wih-win): religious gatherings

migiziins (mih-gih-zeens): eagle

migiziwag (mih-GEE-zih-wag): the plural form of migiziins

mi'iw minik (mih-IW min-ick): exclamation at the end of a story

moningwanay (moh-ning-wah-nay): flicker

Moningwanaykaning (moh-ning-wah-NAY-kan-ing): Island of the Golden-Breasted Woodpecker, also known as Madeline Island, largest of the Apostle Islands in Southern Lake Superior, spiritual home of the Anishinabeg

namadabin (nah-MAH-di-bin): sit down

Nanabozho (nan-ah-boh-ZHO): the great teacher of the Ojibwe, who used his comical human side to teach lessons, often through hilarious mistakes

n'dawnis (in-DAH-nis): my daughter

neebin (nee-bin): summer

neshkey (nesh-kay): look

n'gaa (in-gah): old way of saying mother

nimisay (NIH-MIH-say): younger sister

Nokomis (no-KOH-mis): grandmother

nookoo (noo-koo): shortened version of Nokomis

Odaawa (oh-dah-wah): a tribe related to the Ojibwe

ogimaa (oh-geh-ma): head person, chief, king or queen

ogitchida (oh-GIT-chih-dah): male leader

ogitchidaag (oh-GIT-chih-dahg): the plural form of ogitchida

ogitchidakwe (oh-GIT-chih-dah-kway): female leader

okij (oh-KIHJ): pipe stem

ombay (OM-bay): come here; let's go

omooday (oh-moo-die): bottle

owah (oh-WAH): exclamation of alarm or surprise, like "oh!"

ozhibee'igay (oh-zhi-BEE-ih-gay): writing

peendigen (peen-dig-eyn): come in

pukwe (puck-way): reed used in making mats

sa (sah): part of geget sa; a polite addition to speech

sabeys (sah-bays): net

tikinagun (tick-ih-NAH-gun): a cradle board made of light-weight wood, with a footrest on one end and a bow-shaped frame at the other. A baby is wrapped snugly into the tikinagun with cloth, blankets, and skins. The tikina-gun can be carried on the mother's back, leaned against a tree or a wall, or safely hung from a tree branch. Small toys, such as shells, dream catchers, or pieces of birchbark with bitten designs are often hung from the bow-shaped frame near the baby's head to amuse him or her.

waabooz (WAH-booz): rabbit

waaboozoog (WAH-booz-oog): the plural form of waabooz

weeji'ishin (wee-jih-ih-shin): help me do something

weesinidah (wee-sin-ih-dah): let's eat!

wegonen (way-go-nayn): what?

wesineeg (wee-sin-ig): all of you eat

weweni gagigidoon (way-way-nih gah-gih-gi-doon): speak carefully

weyass (wee-yass): meat

wigwam (WIHG-wahm): a birchbark house

wiindigoo (WIN-di-goo): a giant monster of Ojibwe teachings, often made of ice and associated with the starvation and danger of deep winter

zeegwun (ZEEG-wun): spring

zhaganashimowin (zha-gah-NAHSH-ih-moh-win): white man's language

zhooniyaa (shoo-nih-yah): money

Dear Reader:

I began *The Game of Silence* while I was still writing *The Birchbark House*, on Madeline Island in Lake Superior, where my Ojibwe family originated long ago. The main character, Omakayas, is so very alive to me. I see through her eyes, feel her feelings, catch myself making her expressions as I write. The delicious shock of diving into Lake Superior in midsummer and the smell of fish stew cooking on an open fire are my experiences, too. I like to do the things Omakayas does, just to make sure I am describing them accurately. So I pick mushrooms, explode puffballs, fall asleep next to my dog, and remember how difficult it was to remain quiet as a child.

The title, *The Game of Silence*, is based on a real Ojibwe game adults used to keep children quiet when they needed adult time indoors. As for the illustrations, my children have posed at various ages for photographs that I now keep catalogued in shoeboxes. So I have the added warmth of loving the child I'm drawing. The objects pictured are pieces from my own collection of traditionally made Ojibwe baskets and moccasins.

I take a long time to write these books because they are, in the truest sense, labors of love for my characters, my children, my ancestors, and my people. I hope you enjoyed reading this as much as I enjoyed writing it.

Louise Erdrich

EXTRAS

Ann Marsden

Here I am with my old pal Cola, fiercely goofy, lovable, and also stubborn like me. I wanted my picture taken with him because he is seventeen and he is the inspiration for the dog in *The Game of Silence*.

Meet Louise Erdrich

LOUISE ERDRICH LIVES with her daughters in Minnesota. They have a very new dog, a very strange cat—both pitch black—and a garden devoted to rhubarb. Ms. Erdrich is a member of the Turtle Mountain Band of Ojibwa. She grew up in North Dakota and is of German American and Chippewa descent. As a child, her father would give her a nickel for every story she wrote, and her mother used to make books out of construction paper for Ms. Erdrich to fill with stories. As an adult, she worked as an editor for the Boston Indian Council's newspaper, *Circle*; as a writing instructor, as a poetry teacher in prisons, and as a beet weeder, a waitress, a psychiatric aide, a lifeguard, and a construction flag signaler. She is the author of many critically acclaimed and bestselling novels for adults, including *Love Medicine*, which won the U.S. National Book Critics Circle Award, and more recently *Four Souls* and *The Master Butcher's Singing Club*. She has also written a picture book, *Grandmother's Pigeon*. *The Game of Silence* continues the story of Omakayas begun in *The Birchbark House*, which was nominated for the National Book Award for Young People's Literature, and which was inspired when Ms. Erdrich and her mother, Rita Gourneau Erdrich, were researching their own family history. Ms. Erdrich is planning to write seven more books about Omakayas and her family, and the stories will span a hundred years of history.

We Asked Louise Erdrich . . .

Where do you go for inspiration?
Home.

What is your idea of perfect happiness?
Daughters.

Which book do you wish you'd written?
The New Testament.

What are your favorite children's books?
The Golden Books Treasury of Elves and Fairies, illustrated by Garth Williams, now out of print. My mother found me a copy on eBay. I love *My Father's Dragon*, the Redwall series, anything by Patricia Wrede, Philip Pullman, or Tamora Pierce. I love The Dark Is Rising series and *A Wrinkle in Time*.

What objects do you carry with you?
Round stones.

Do you have any pet peeves?
Loud, persistent buzzing noises of mechanical origin. And I don't like that feeling you get when fingers and toes half freeze, then warm up and tingle with pain.

Which living person(s) do you most admire?
My mother and father.

What's the best compliment you've ever received?
Mom, you are my *best* mom!

What would be your desert island luxury?
A dictionary, but that's more a necessity. For a luxury, I'd choose vanilla ice cream—hard to get on a desert island.

What was your favorite pastime when you were younger?
Predictably, I loved to read. But I was the oldest and had lots of chores. I hid my library books everywhere so I could read all over the house. Sometimes I would *not* come when I was called. I played outdoors all the time, built snow forts, swam, climbed a thousand trees, tamed a baby raccoon and loved my brothers and sisters. I had a lucky childhood.

Did you always want to be a writer?
My father paid me a nickel for every story I wrote as a kid. That bought a Popsicle. I loved Popsicles, especially grape. Perhaps my entire career is based on grape Popsicles.

What are you writing at the moment?
I just started the third book in this series, *Twelve Moons Running*. It is about the year (Twelve Moons) that Omakayas and her family spend on the move. It is a year of adventure—which is to say full of some harrowing difficulties. Adventures often come with risk. In the first chapter, Pinch gets a new name when he is hit by a porcupine that he knocks out of a tree. Quill boy. Omakayas survives running a flooded rapids in the dark and begins to understand that she is growing up. I'd like to tell you more, but I have to write it first.

THE BELOVED HOME OF OMAKAYAS AND A MAP OF HER ADVENTURES DURING THE YEAR OF THE GAME OF SILENCE

c. 1849

THE SHORE WHERE THE RAGGEDY ONES APPEARED

WHERE OMAKAYAS MET HER SPIRIT, ALONE

THE CHURCH WHERE DEYDEY VISITED FATHER BARAGA

THE CABIN OF OLD TALLOW

THE MISSION AND HOME OF THE BREAK-APART GIRL

THE WINTER CABIN

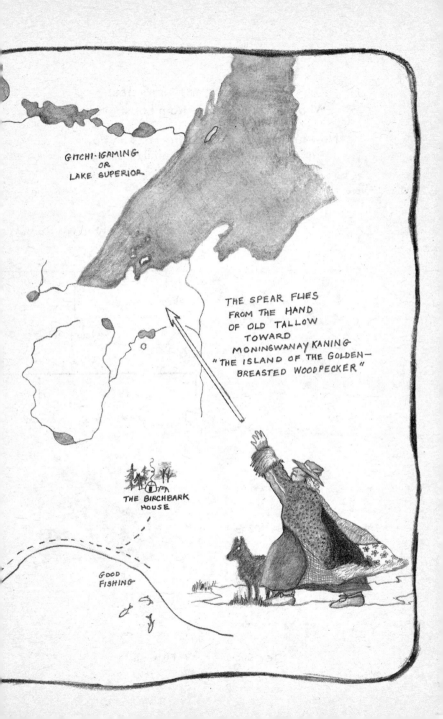

This is Omakayas's family tree.
Who do you recognize from her story?

Now turn the page for instructions on how to make your very own family tree!

Old Tallow = = = = Hat

Nokomis = = = = nahbam (husband)

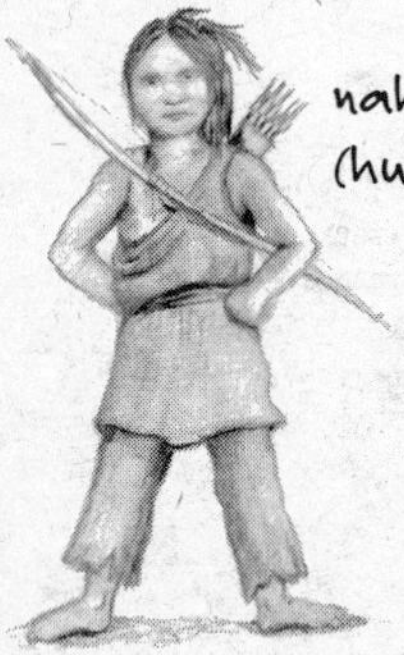

nah bam = = = = Akewaynzee
(husband)

Yellow Kettle = = =

Two-Strike Girl

(2)Angeline Omakayas Pinch

LEGEND

= = = Traditional Ojibwe marriage

| Children born from any of the above unions

¦ Adopted children

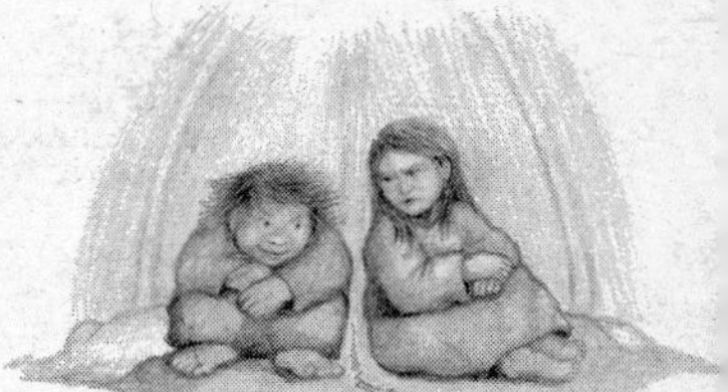

Ten Snow = = = = Fishtail

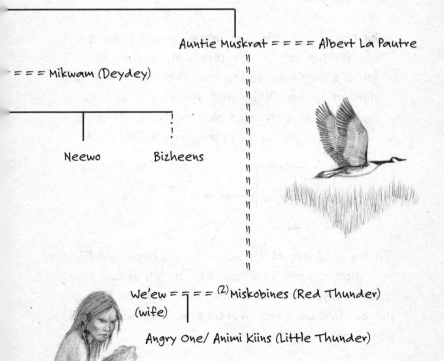

Auntie Muskrat = = = = Albert La Pautre

= = = Mikwam (Deydey)

Neewo   Bizheens

We'ew = ┬ = = (2) Miskobines (Red Thunder)
(wife) |

Angry One/ Animi Kiins (Little Thunder)

Make Your Own Family Tree!

WHEN MAKING A family tree, keep these simple rules in mind:

boxes for boys, ☐ circles for girls, ◯ and short lines —— connect two people if they have children together.

1. First, you'll write in your grandparents. Draw a box on the top left of the page. Write your father's father's name inside the box. Draw a circle to the right of the box. Write your father's mother's name inside the circle. Now connect the box and the circle with a short line (because they have kids!).

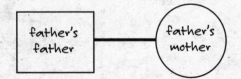

On the right side of the page, draw a circle and fill in your mother's mother's name. To the left of that, draw a box with your mother's father's name inside. Connect this box and circle with a short line. That takes care of your grandparents!

2. Now you can start on your parents' branches, which will include your parents and your aunts and uncles. From the middle of the line connecting your father's parents, draw a line going straight down. If your father has any brothers or sisters, at the bottom of this line draw another line going from left to right. Then draw short downward lines to show how many children your father's parents had.

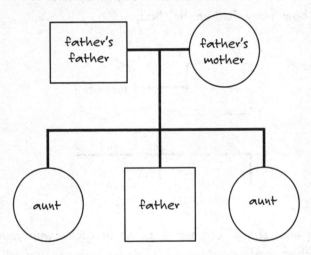

If your grandparents on your father's side had three children, then you will have three lines branching off. The lines should connect to boxes or circles with your father's brothers' and sisters' names inside (including your father's!). Start with the oldest to the youngest, going from left to right. If your father is an only child, the downward line should just end in a box with your father's name in it.

Repeat this on your mother's side.

3. Now you're ready for your section of the tree! As you did above, draw a line connecting your father and your mother. In the middle of this line, draw a downward line. If they had more than one child, at the bottom of this downward line draw a line going from left to right. Then draw short downward lines to show how many children they had.

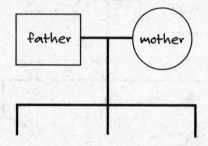

The lines should connect to boxes or circles with your brothers' and sisters' names inside (including your own!). Remember, start with the oldest to the youngest, going from left to right. If you are an only child, the downward line should just end in one box (if you're a boy) or one circle (if you're a girl) with your name in it.

And now your family tree is complete.

For added fun, you can write in the years that people were born (so if your grandfather was born in 1935, then write "1935" in brackets just below his name). You can also add your cousins by connecting your aunts and uncles and showing how many children they had. But watch out! You may have to extend your family tree on other pieces of paper.

Have fun! This is your chance to discover how everyone is related and teach the rest of your family about their own history.